THE GAME

BY ROBERT FALCONERO

DORRANCE
PUBLISH NG CO
EST. 1920
PITTSBURGH, PENNSYLVANIA 15238

Dorrance Publishing Co
585 Alpha Drive
Suite 103
Pittsburgh, PA 15238
Visit our website at *www.dorrancebookstore.com*

ISBN: 978-1-6495-7112-0
eISBN: 978-1-6495-7610-1

I dedicate this book to my loving wife, Mary

THE GAME

CHAPTER 1

FLOOR TO CEILING DARK OAK PANELS bearing oil paintings of men in business suits graced the walls of the smoke-filled room. Only one of the four overhead green shaded lights shined through the haze, like a light house beacon cutting through a fog. An eerie green glow illuminated the end of the thirty-foot-long mahogany table with silhouettes of empty red leather chairs seated on both sides like soldiers at attention. Ash trays containing smoldering cigar butts were randomly situated along the long shiny table, and seated under the green glow were two animated figures.

In the chairman's seat at the head of the table sat a tall, lanky, middle-aged man in a Harris Tweed three-piece suit, his entire body crouched over, half glasses sitting on the end nose, rapidly reading and signing documents that were placed in from of him by a young woman in a blue business suit. A stack of documents sat in front of her, and as soon as he completed one, she would remove the signed one and feed him another with an unthinking and methodical motion. He would silently check his watch every two or three documents and then focus on the new piece of paper that was shoved in front of him by this robot-like female. The only noise in the room was the sound of the nib of his Mount Blanc pen scratching out his signature on the contracts in a production line type of motion.

He suddenly stopped, ran his hand through his already disheveled hair, pushed the glasses from the tip of his nose to the bridge, and carefully read the attached cover letter for a second time.

He quickly stood up, removed his glasses, and threw them down the long shiny table, and while they were still in motion, yelled, "We will continue to provide services in the usual efficient manner? In the usual efficient manner? In the usual manner? The usual! USUAL! God damn it nothing is USUAL!"

He banged his fist on the table, causing many of the ash trays to lift as though they were propelled by an earth tremor. The woman nervously began fumbling her papers, not knowing what to do, pulling her chair away from him more towards the corner of the table, her eyes darting back and forth between him and the door, planning her exit if he became more violent in either his words or actions.

He stood and stared into the darkness at the other end of the room, his eyes filled with rage, and his hand still pounding the table. "There is nothing usual in life, nothing is usual in business...things are the synthesis of unusual thesis and antithesis..."

He turned to her and pointed his long skinny finger at her, waved it, and yelled, "Would it be usual if you made it home tonight? Would it be usual if you didn't die in your sleep tonight? Answer me! Would it or would it not?"

She didn't know what to say, her eyes filled with tears more from the fear of not knowing what this mad man was going to do next based upon her answer. Lie leaned over and his steely blue eyes stared into hers, his eyebrows were scrunched as though they were poised in anticipation, his body was shaking nervously, and his finger was still waving in front of her nose as though it were suspended from a ceiling hung mobile.

"Well, young lady, are you a mute...now answer me!" he yelled with his face only inches from hers. As she began to get up to flee, he stopped her chair with his hand and said, "I want this god dammed contract cancelled today...do you understand? I want you to go and type a cancellation letter now...and I want that letter hand delivered to this son of a bitch. Is this a local company?"

"Yes, it is a local company, Mr. Bigelow," she said nervously as she attempted to compose herself, slowly wiping the tears from the corners of her eyes and glancing at the letterhead on the contract.

"Then I want the cancellation letter hand delivered within the hour, and I want you to deliver it!" he shouted as he abruptly sat in the waiting leather chair, pushing the chair back some two to three feet from the impact of his thrust.

"Whom shall I say cancelled the contract?" she asked as she pulled out her steno pad, grabbed the contract from where he had tossed it, and nervously began writing down his instructions.

"The Board, tell them the Board decided," he stated as he resumed signing contracts. "Now go and do it!" he yelled, pointing at the door without looking up.

CHAPTER 2

BURSTS OF MORNING LIGHT FLASHED into his car as he drove past budding maple trees. The sun shining sporadically from behind out-stretched branches caused a strobe-like effect that was almost hypnotic. Jason rubbed his eyes and rolled down his window as a blast of cool morning spring air ruffled his hair and tingled his face. He flattened his hair with his hand and then turned up his disk player. Blaring was Bach's Brandenburg's Series one and two. Somehow playing this tape on the short ten-minute ride from his home to his office seemed to energize him. It was as though all of the synapses in his brain connected at the same time, sending colorful images onto a large visual screen in his mind. The music heightened his awareness of everything around him. Bach reached across 350 years of time and put him into an Alpha state. Whenever his kids drove with him, which was very seldom, they would switch off his disc player and put on some rap singer. Jason could only compare this sound to a level of dementia achievable only after an individual received either an involuntary blow to the cerebral cortex or a lobotomy performed with a Black and Decker drill.

He could smell freshly cut grass combined with car fumes as he turned onto Route 195. Groups of young college students dressed in orange vests were in the median strip cutting grass and picking up bottles along with crushed Mc-

Donald's bags that apparently had been tossed out of someone's car window over the weekend. He turned his head sideways and caught the glimpse of a cute blonde who was leaning on a rake and talking to a group of pimply-faced teen aged boys who were also leaning on rakes.

"They had apparently picked up her scent and were responding to the call of their overactive glands," he thought as he approached them. Jason remembered that at their age, he used to get sexually aroused just fantasying about Betty Crocker. So he could understand how this beautiful creature in tight blue jeans with strands of flowing blond mane blowing in the wind could attract a pack of testosterone riddled adolescents.

He turned his head from front to side again just to make sure that he was still on the road. She noticed his attention, smiled, and waved to him as he accelerated from the entrance to the passing lane, cutting off three lanes of speeding highway traffic. Brakes screeched and horns blasted, but his attention was not focused on the fact that he was almost turned into luncheon meat, his attention was on the blond siren.

He adjusted his rear-view mirror just in time to see her put both hands up to her head in an apparent gesture of one who had almost witnessed a death. Also in the rear-view mirror were two of the drivers with their arms extended out of rolled down windows—throwing him fingers as an obvious sign of their displeasure with his driving skills, or lack thereof. He thought God, she's about the same age as my daughter.

He drove only a short distance before he took the Fall River exit. His office was in Fall River. He would have preferred to be in Boston, but his wife was from that area and the cost of living was cheap. He referred to the city as the Dead Zone. Intellectually, culturally, and spiritually devoid is what he would say to his partner.

His partner John, who was born and raised in Fall River, would get defensive at Jason's snide remarks and would ask him, "Then why do you stay here?"

Jason's answer was always the same. He'd go on a diatribe. "In this city, I am an intellectual giant, a genius among morons, a leader among followers, an inspiration among the downtrodden, and a shining light in the ever present darkness. In Boston or New York, I'd merely be a grain of sand on a large beach, but here I am the rock of Gibraltar in a child's sand box."

Jason would always end his pontificating by saying, "John, you know what the problem in this community is? The problem is that in this city, there are more horses asses than there are horses."

John, whose stomach overlapped his pants, without saying a word would throw Jason a figure, tuck his shirt into his partially visible belt, which really emphasized his belly, and walk away moving his head from side to side.

When those occasions arose when Jason had to meet a prospective client, needed a three-martini lunch, or just discretely wanted to meet a female companion... Boston was the place. How often those occasions arose was dependent upon the level of pressure being exerted on him in any given day. Occasionally he would take his partner John on some of his Boston jaunts but preferred to make the trips alone. Boston was a safe zone because even though it was only fifty miles north of Fall River, most people in that community had never been there. To many of them, their world ended at the city line. Therefore the likelihood of running into a familiar face was extremely remote.

When Jay was not in the office by ten o'clock, John just assumed that he had something or someone lined up in Boston. Although neither talked about Jason's missing day, credit card returns from the Four Seasons Hotel and Anthony's Pier Four Restaurant confirmed his whereabouts.

Only once did John question his eccentric behavior. A billing from American Express showed a flight for one to Brazil on a Friday with a return flight on Monday. The total cost of that getaway was $7,500. That little trip nearly dissolved their partnership, not to mention Jay's marriage. Somehow with Jason's charismatic personality, or his line of bullshit as John called it, he managed to keep both in place, although it was nearly a month before he decided to spontaneously disappear again. This time to Providence, which was only twenty minutes away... and for only one day.

These little get always were interpreted by his wife Marnie as a safety valve. Being a devout Catholic, she looked at these little interruptions in Jason's work week as a sort of retreat. A time when he could meditate and rejuvenate his creative batteries and come back a better person.

She would tell John, "You know he's a hard worker and he needs his private time."

With a skeptical look on his face, John would respond by saying, "Marnie, you are a saint. He doesn't deserve you. Both you and Mother Teresa will probably be canonized." John knew that on many of those little retreats, Jason would spend the entire day going from strip joint to strip joint in Boston's Combat Zone...spending hundreds of dollars on cheap champagne, on cheap hookers. He wouldn't come back with his batteries charged... He'd return needing a jump start.

Jay would spend between seventy-five and one hundred hours a week working in his office and missed just about every event that required his presence as a father. His two kids really didn't know him, nor did he know them.

Somehow he felt comfortable with that arrangement, as long as he knew that his wife would cover for him and make positive excuses for absences.

"Your dad is working tonight, so that you can have your horses, attend private school, and continue living in our beautiful home and..." she'd tell them while wiping their tears and cursing him inside.

Now and then he'd think about the day when he would be on his death bed, hooked up to a respirator, and the decision of whether to pull the plug or not would have to be made by his daughters. With total indifference, they would probably say...pull it...as they would to a total stranger, which is what he would be to them.

More upsetting to him would be the decision of whether or not he should be placed in a nursing home when his kids no longer thought that he was capable of taking care of himself. He dreaded this one more than the plug pulling thought. He could visualize this as being an emotionless decision. By then his kids probably would not even consider taking his elderly ass into their home and caring for him. Would either of them want a total stranger living with them and sharing food with their families?

He deduced that if and when that time arrived, those decisions would be taken care of with money. He would not be dependent upon anyone. With patient assisted suicide being accepted by the courts and the Roe vs. Wade decision upheld, he thought that by then euthanasia would probably be legal.

Maybe his kids would snuff him out for the inheritance? By then they could probably do it legally.

But with money, he would have the means to avoid putting life or death decisions in the hands of his family. Money was his answer to most everything. Having been raised without it gave him an obsession of not only making it but spending it on conspicuous displays of self and family aggrandizement.

His bouts of conspicuous consumption resulted in the purchase of his and hers gold Rolex watches for he and his wife, the acquisition of the Holden Mansion, one of Fall River's most distinguished opulent symbols of the by-gone textile era of the 1850's, a collection of expensive cars, a winter place in Orlando, collections of every electronic gadget on the market, and a wardrobe of designer clothes that made Bloomingdale's look like the Salvation Army.

Frank, Jason's father whose depression experience turned him into what Jason called the eternal pessimist, warned Jay time and time again about planning for the future. Jay would just buy him an expensive gift and tell him not to worry.

"Carpe diem, Pop," Jason would say. "Seize the day."

As Jason pulled into the entrance to the parking deck next to his office, he rolled down his window and said to the man in the attendant's booth, "Good morning, Carlos, nice day."

"Mister Burns. I'm afraid that someone's in your spot," said Carlos rather reluctantly.

"What do you mean, someone is in my spot! I pay you good dammed money to keep that spot open for me, now what the hell happened?" shouted Jason as he pushed his hair off of his forehead while turning his head forward.

"Well, the car was already in the spot when I got here. I, well, I mean…"

Screeching tires and black smoke interrupted Carlos as Jason sped into the dimly lit deck, nearly hitting an oncoming car that was exiting.

"Why do I have to deal with these fucking idiots?" he said to himself as he pulled into an available spot on the fourth floor and slammed on his brakes, nearly hitting the cement wall. He got out and slammed the door while still swearing to himself.

While getting off of the elevator, he could smell the coffee brewing. Linda, his secretary, always got in about a half hour earlier than everyone else and put a fresh pot on. She would do it at this location because she felt safe coming in at this hour, even though the building was vacant. Unlike their former location, this office building was recently refurbished and was located in the heart of the city.

Jason's company, The Creative Factory, occupied about one half of the fourth floor. Because he was the largest tenant, the landlord let him select the gray and mauve color scheme in the hall way and offices. Somehow gray and burgundy never tickled his fancy, but his secretary convinced him that the color combination was state of the art...used in top advertising offices in New York and LA. Since she had never been to either city, he knew that she was lying but went along with her just to keep the peace.

As he approached his office door, he could still smell the new hall rug. He liked the smell. It was like the smell of the interior of a new car. It was probably the formaldehyde, and it was probably killing him every day, but he liked it anyway. Jason had this thing about pollution.

He reasoned that if pollution was so bad for you, and it was much more prevalent today than say seventy-five years ago, then why are we living to be ninety today when people died at twenty-seven then? He particularly enjoyed diesel fumes. When he was a kid, he enjoyed walking in back of a bus as it accelerated from a complete stop. He was not exactly an environmentalist...as a matter of fact, the only thing green that he enjoyed was money.

"You're looking great today," smiled Jason at Linda, who was sitting in front a computer screen and typing what appeared to be a letter.

"Good morning, Jay," said Linda without missing a key stroke. He liked Linda. She was middle aged but never tried to cover up that fact or pretended that she was something other. Her hair was salt and pepper. Mostly salt. Her clothing was conservative, and her knowledge of how to operate an office is what Jason called the mooring of his business. He compared himself and the rest of his staff as bouncing, wandering boats with guide ropes that were attached to Linda. She was the only one in that office who was anchored. She did all of the necessary mundane things, like preparing payroll, paying taxes, and paying the utility bills. Her attention to the day to day minutia allowed the free spirits of the Creative Factory the time and space they needed to create without being impinged by the real world.

After four or five glasses of Asti Spumonte at their last holiday party, she told Jason that she looked at him, John, and the rest of the staff as loose cannons.

She asked, "Can I talk to you freely… I mean it's almost Christmas Eve…you people are the strangest collection of characters that I have ever worked for. Don't get me wrong, I mean.. " After noticing a glimpse of disapproval in Jay's watery, half inebriated eyes, she qualified herself by saying, "Creative loose cannons…yes…very creative… I mean really nice strange characters…no, I mean…nice people…"

Jay laughed and filled her glass again and said, "Tell me more," which of course she didn't.

"Any calls for me?" asked Jason as he entered his office.

"None yet," said Linda above the clicking of computer keys.

"Listen, when Mr. Kamoto arrives, just send him into the conference room. Is John here yet?"

"He's in his office. He was in when I got in. He may have spent the night," said Linda without turning her head away from the computer screen.

The office contained a fold out bed that either Jay or John used when their work took them into the early hours of the morning. Often times when the creative juices began flowing, the two of them would send out for Chinese, sit on the conference room table in lotus positions, and toss ideas around as professional baseball players would toss around pitches.

There were occasions when deadlines had to be met and the two of them were on a roll, when they would work thirty-six to forty hours straight. Jason would stretch out on the floor with his eyes half opened while John would recite from the telephone book yellow pages or anything else that he had available. John called these moments "mental filibustering." He felt that as long as the mind was receptive to words, thoughts would automatically flow. These interchanges of words kept their two minds connected, even though fatigue threatened to shut them down. When they were in these creative moods, Jason felt that their minds would meet on a spiritual plane where pure energy was their only existence. It was a marriage of energy whose off spring were ideas that were whispered, yelled, or moaned as though they were speaking in tongues.

All of these verbal expressions were recorded by two voice activated tape recorders that were latter transcribed by Linda. They learned that without the recorders, many ideas were lost forever as they would latter sit and unsuccessfully try and reconstruct them.

John was initially opposed to the use of recorders because he felt that whomever transcribed the tapes were privied to some secret ritual between he and Jason. John would compare their sessions to a Masonic meeting. Words and symbols that were only understood by those brethren who were properly trained and initiated in the sacred rite. For, in John's opinion, it was only the brethren who understood the tremendous importance of the ritual and allegories. To the cowen and eavesdroppers, a Masonic meeting would appear to be silly and incomprehensible.

Convincing John was no easy task. It occurred after a marathon session in which both of them were so tired and exhausted that many of the selling points of the campaign that they had discussed and agreed on were lost to fatigue.

Jason left in disgust after leaving a note on John's desk that read, "The fawn that exists in the mind, leaves no tracks in the snow." Recorders were used during their next session.

Linda would kid each one about their eccentricities. She found them amusing and puzzling. She once asked Jason why he wore two watches, and he explained by saying that the measurement of time was an invention of man. Since the human race decided to be connected to a specific time frame, he felt that if his primary watch failed that he would be lost forever in time. As he saw it, the back-up watch guaranteed him continuity within this time frame. When Linda first heard this story, she thought that Jason was putting her on, but she knew that he was serious the day that both watches failed.

After she responded to his intercom, she found him crouched in the corner of his office with his head tucked between his legs, his head covered with one arm, the other extended clutching two watches in his hand, and yelling, "They're broken…get me two more now…quickly…these are broken"

She ran down to the drug store and bought him two Timex's until she could get his two expensive watches fixed. He wore a Cartier on his left wrist and a Rolex on his right. As she ran out of the room, she thought that with $15,000 worth of wrist watches, you'd think that at least one of them worked properly. Then again…she thought, maybe he didn't wind them. She was hoping that he would tell her to throw them out, but as she said latter to her friend…he's not that crazy. She never discussed the watch incident with Jason and just carried on as though what had occurred was normal. Even if she had discussed it with him, Jason always seemed to come up with a plausible explanation for his strange quirks.

She could never forget the morning that Jason came into work looking as though he had been shot out of a canon. "Tough night last night?" she pryingly asked him, hoping to solicit some juicy gossip.

"Can I talk to you alone, Linda?" he asked as he signaled her to come into his office. He told her a story about telepathically receiving a message that space visitors were scheduled to make contact with him the day before. He stood in the parking lot next to his home until three in the morning. He then decided to take his car and go riding in the country with the hope of having an encounter with the aliens similar to Barney Hill's. He explained to her that he rode around until 4:30 in the morning when suddenly his car was filled with light. He told her that he thought that that was it…that he would probably be calling in to the office long distance. That if John thought the Brazilian trip was something, wait until he got an intergalactic credit card slip on this one.

Well, Jason said the light was a blue light…a flashing blue light…and after making him walk a straight line and giving him a breathalyzer test…he escorted him back to his home and waited until he was in the house with the lights off.

Linda never repeated this story to anyone because she knew that her husband would probably make her quit.

John, on the other hand, was a bit more subtle in his eccentricities. He wore the same tie every day along with different colored socks and never felt that it was necessary to explain any of his oddities. Even Jason knew him well enough to accept everything that he did at its face value rather than get into unexplainable areas. When she first met him, she once jokingly told John that his tie was getting a little gamey. He then ignored her for over a week. After that incident, she never dared mention any of his oddities again. At least not to his face.

As Jason entered John's office, he was not behind his desk but instead was sitting on a couch reading a bound report.

"Is that the Kamoto proposal?" Jason asked as he opened the vertical blinds to the morning sun that filled the room with a blast of white light. John always kept them closed, and his office reminded him of a catacomb. His disdain for the sun was reflected in his white waxy complexion that never changed from season to season.

"Yes, now please close the fucking blinds," John shouted as he raised the report to shield his eyes.

"You're liked a god damned vampire for Christ sake. Now why do you look puzzled, is there anything wrong with our presentation?" asked Jason.

"No, everything is fine, just remember to tell him that all of this stuff is time dated and that this marketing campaign must be launched within the next two weeks in order to take advantage of the window of opportunity," said John while lowering the report from his face as Jason yanked on the pull string, drawing the long white vertical blinds closed.

"Did Linda make enough copies? And what about the slide presentation… did she set it up in the conference room? And the tea…the Japanese tea… I told her to rent an Oriental serving set if she had to…I want Kamoto to feel comfortable. As far as this time dated issue, I don't think that we should push it…" said Jason as he paced back and forth in from of the couch.

"Jay, we've had eleven meetings with this son of a bitch. We need this contract and we need it now…we've already invested too much time and effort into this to let this nonsense spill over into a twelfth meeting. Either shit or get off the pot," said John as he rose and tossed the report on the top of his desk that was strewn with everything, from last week's Boston Globe to a half-eaten sandwich that was covered with green mold.

Jason first looked at one watch and then at the other and said, "Kamato is five minutes late. In eleven meetings, the man has never been late."

John smilingly said, "Yeah, maybe his Japanese car broke down, or maybe his Seiko shit the bed."

"Jason, seriously, let's not blow this one...we need this account...remember the McKennsey..." said John while scratching his forehead with his right hand.

"Please, John," interrupted Jason at the top of his voice while throwing his report across the desk. "Don't mention the McKenzie proposal again, I'm sick of hearing it! How many times do you want me to tell you that I shouldn't have procrastinated, I shouldn't have yelled at their public relations person, even though she was an asshole, and I shouldn't have done such a sloppy job on our presentation! I'm sorry! You've already nailed me to the fucking cross a thousand times; what do you want me to do, cut out my heart and put it on the fucking desk? Is that what you want from me?" said Jason, opening his suit coat and pointing to his chest.

"No, I don't want your heart. What I want is this deal to go through. With Hong Kong closing its doors in 1997, this account could be just the beginning of a deluge of a lot of foreign dollars. Kamato has a number of firms in Hong Kong in addition to his companies in Japan. Japanese yen, British pounds. Hong Kong yen, and American bucks. We can do it. Let's just work very closely today to pull this thing off and get this badly needed account." John extended his hand as an act of friendship and cohesion.

Jason extended his hand and grabbed John's. He then pulled him close and gave him a bear hug.

"Let's knock 'em dead, partner, let's make 1993 a banner year," said Jason while slapping John on the back.

Just then the door to the office swung open and Linda poked her head in and said, "Am I interrupting anything? If I am, me and Kamato will go out and get some egg rolls and leave you two alone.'

"Want to join us, Lin, we'll make it a threesome?" smiled John as he winked at her while reaching for his suit coat.

"Nah. I'll pass on this one, guys, do you want me to tell our guest that you'll be right with him?"

"Thanks, Lin, we'll be right out," said Jason as he picked up his report and headed for the door.

The conference room was designed by Jason and was actually a plate glass encapsulated room containing an elliptical conference table with eight modern chairs. On the door, painted in bright red letters, were the words "Think Tank." This glass rectangle, situated in the middle of the entire office complex resembled either a fish tank or an animal observation pen. Somehow the boys, as Linda referred to them, felt very comfortable working in the tank.

Jason and John watched Mr. Kamato pouring himself a cup of tea as they approached the think room's glass door.

Before entering Jason turned to John and said, "When I'm ready for your portion, I'll have Linda buzz you."

John patted him on the back, reached for the glass door knob, and said, "Good luck in there."

Jason just nodded his head and entered.

"Kanishewa," said Jason while bowing his head.

"And a good morning to you also," said Mr. Kamato, also bowing his head.

After a round of handshakes, the two sat down and began discussing the marketing plan. Out of the corner of her eye, Linda watched them through the glass panels while pretending to be entering data into the computer. Kamato would be their first big client in over four years, and she knew the importance of the meeting. She did their books, paid their bills, and prepared their financial statements and knew and understood how frail this struggling company was.

Suddenly she looked forward and standing in front of her desk was a stunning young women in a blue business suit with a brown envelope in her hand.

Startled she snapped her head backwards and said, "Oh my God, where did you come from? I didn't even hear you come into the office."

"I'm sorry if I frightened you, but I have an urgent message for Jason Burns. Can I possibly see him right now?"

"I'm sorry he cannot be disturbed, he's in a very important meeting," said Linda, pointing toward the glass enclosure, "but I'll give him your message."

"Is that Mr. Burns in there?" asked the woman pointing toward the glass wall and walking toward the glass door.

Linda got up and stood in front of the woman, blocking her way, and said, "Yes, that's him, but you cannot go in there. Say, just who are you and what do you want?"

The woman stopped just inches from Linda's erect body and said, "My name is Sheila Cochrane, and I am the Executive Secretary to Flagstaff International. Now I was told to personally deliver this message," she said, waving the brown envelope in front of her. "Now if you don't mind, I will do my job." She forged ahead, pushing Linda aside and proceeding towards the glass door.

Linda grabbed her by the arm and stopped her and said forcefully, "I'll call the police if I must. But you are not going into that conference room. Now do you understand me?"

Jason, who was watching the woman through the glass panel from the time that she entered the office, saw Linda grab her arm and knew that there was some sort of a problem. He excused himself and moved quickly toward the door. Once that he was out of the conference room, he extended his arms and moved the two women away from Kamato's view.

Once they were on the other side of the room, he dropped his arms and asked the woman, "Who in the hell are you and what the hell are you doing?"

"Jay, she says that she has an urgent message for you that she had to hand deliver personally," said Linda, pointing toward the brown envelope in the woman's hand.

Angrily grabbing the envelope, he mumbled, "Well, let me see if it's urgent enough to interrupt the most important meeting that I've had in the past three months."

He tore the top of the envelope open and removed the letter and read it while the two women watched.

He dropped his hand containing the letter, looked the woman in the eyes, and questioned, "Are you serious? This is a joke, isn't it? I mean who, who sent you? Is this from one of my competitors? This is absurd!"

"Jay, do you want me to call security?" asked Linda while reaching for the phone.

"Mr. Burns, I'm sorry... I had nothing to do with it," said the woman while walking toward the outer door. "It was a Board decision. I merely typed it and was given the unfortunate assignment of delivering it. Again I'm sorry."

The woman walked abruptly out of the office and left Jay standing there, staring into space.

"Jay, can I read the letter?" asked Linda who was rubbing her brow, while fumbling for her cigarettes in her purse. She wasn't allowed to smoke in the office, but felt that this was probably an exception to the rule.

Jason threw the letter on the desk in front of Linda and said, "Lin, I can't go back into that room right now. My stride has been broken. I can't possibly go in there, smile, joke, think, and sell my soul until I get to the bottom of this. I'm sure that this is a cruel joke and...."

Linda interrupted by saying, "Oh my God, they cancelled. They cancelled their contract."

"Lin, I know, I can read. Please I just can't go back in there. I've got to get to the bottom of...."

"My God, they cancelled...our biggest contract has been cancelled..." moaned Linda, sounding almost like a professional mourner at an Irish funeral.

"Jay, you've got to get back into that meeting, our biggest contract has just been cancelled," said Linda while pointing toward the glass panel. "It's now up to you."

"Linda, I'll be in my office. I can't go back in there. I've got to get to the bottom of this. Please put John on the phone intercom and tell him that he is on his own and that I am suddenly not feeling very well, which is not far from the truth. After that get me the Flagstaff Company on the phone. Let me talk with Saunders from the marketing department. Jesus Christ, I don't understand... they loved our work..." mumbled Jason as he walked toward his office with his head hung down.

The intercom buzzed twice before Jason reached for the button. "Jay, its Saunders on line one," whispered Linda who was also trying to talk to John, who was impatiently standing in from of her.

"Saunders, what the hell is going on over there?" said Jason with a wavy tone of anxiety in his voice.

"Uh, I'm not sure, Jay. I got a copy of your letter about an hour ago... Jay, it was a Board decision... I had nothing to do with it, believe me. I made a few internal calls, but I was told to leave it alone. If I find out anything, I'll let know."

"What do you mean you'll let me know? That's it? No explanation, just forget it? Tom, we've being doing business with Flagstaff for five years now...every campaign produced results that far exceeded projections...that far exceeded anyone's wildest imagination...there were campaigns that were comparable to Madison avenue firms... Tom, what the fuck is going on.... You are my main account..." blurted Jason nervously while tapping a pencil on his desk.

"Jay, I don't know what to ...."

"Tom, don't bullshit me! I deserve an answer! Was it the last campaign... yes, it was, wasn't it? The theme was wrong, wasn't it... I should have listened to John...he said that the space theme with the astronauts took a giant leap outside of your product line... He was right... I should have..."

"Jay, your last campaign was brilliant...it was a stroke of genius...it was probably deserving of a Cleo award...Since then four of our competitors have created advertising campaigns similar to yours...our sales increased by a full three percentage points right after its release..." said Tom.

"Then for Christ's sake, Tom...why were we cancelled... I must know...." Jay dropped his pencil and ruffled his hair while leaning back in his office chair and staring at the florescent light.

"Uh, I just want you to know what this means... You...you...are my bread and butter....without you I will probably....'

"Jay, you have other accounts... Flagstaff will probably return to you after they realize the impact of what they have done...stay with your other accounts until then," said Tom.

"Tom, this is effective today...can they do that, I mean I really haven't looked at the escape clause on the contract because I never thought that it would end this way...but do you think that your company can just cancel?" asked Jay, who was now pacing in front of his desk. the curly telephone receiver cord pulled to its limit.

"Jay, its legal, I checked the contract just before I called you. As a matter of fact, it was your attorney who insisted on such loose escape language. Don't you remember when we negotiated the deal?" asked Tom, whose voice now reflected a hint of impatience.

"Tom, I'm sunk," said Jay with a quiver in his voice.

"Jay, now pull yourself together..."

Jay was now weeping openly on the other end of the line, covering the receiver with his hand as he tried disparately to compose himself. Tom was still talking, but it sounded as though all of his words were blended together.

Rather than humiliate himself any further, he gently placed the telephone receiver back onto the telephone. He turned his chair around and looked out of the window...his vision was focused on a seagull that was just about to land on the upper span of the Braga Bridge. Its tiny body kept on getting caught in the up-draft that was blowing off of the dark blue-green Taunton River some 200 feet below.

Every time that it tried to land, a blast of air pushed its little body backwards, its wings flapping in an attempt at gaining some equilibrium. Finally after four attempts and out of frustration, it aborted its efforts and flew off towards shore. Just then the door to his office flew open and slammed against the wall with such force that the door knob penetrated the wall board in back of it.

Slamming the door shut so hard that a framed diploma came crashing to the floor, John shouted, "Can you tell me just what the hell you think you are doing? We lost the fucking deal... Kimota just walked out in a huff...didn't even say good-bye...you asshole, he was our ace in the hole!"

"Didn't you tell him that I was sick?" said Jason while rubbing the residue of tears from his eyes.

"You expected him to buy that flimsy excuse... you were just in there as healthy as a horse, plowing through your presentation as though the Russians were in Newport, and suddenly you leave the room...to make matters worse, you politely excused yourself and left the room smiling. The last thing that you say to Kimota is that you'll be right back. And then you don't return. This was your presentation! My contribution was merely to present the figures at the end. You were responsible for the creative part, the part that Kimota came to listen to," yelled John while loosening his tie and tossing his coat on the floor somewhere near the coat hook.

"John, he'll be back, I've got some bad news, much worse than yours."

"In the pig's ass he'll be back. He dumped the entire presentation into the wastepaper basket on the way out and was mumbling something in Japanese as he was doing it. Don't you understand, this is a cultural thing. You insulted the son of a bitch twice in the same day!" exclaimed John as he threw himself onto Jason's office couch. "First you walked out on him and then you didn't return. Are you brained dead, going through your mid-life crisis, or maybe you just don't give a shit!"

"John, read this," said Jason, handing him the folded correspondence.

A puzzled and grimaced look took over John's face as he swung his hand, yanked the letter out of Jason's hand, and quickly read it. The correspondence then fell out of his trembling hand and slowly drifted to the rug while his complexion turned to ashen gray.

"Jay, is this what arrived during the meeting?"

"Yes, it was hand delivered by some Flagstaff secretary. She was apparently instructed to hand it to me personally," said Jason, moving forward in his chair and resting his elbows on his desk while cradling his head.

"Shit, I can understand now why you didn't want to return to the meeting. Jay, we're dead. Without this contract, we're dead. Did you call that weeney... Saunders, Tom Saunders?"

"John, there is nothing that he can do about it. It's out of his hands. The cancellation is legit, and it's effective today. We're dead in the water. We've got one more check coming in from Flagstaff and that's it for our cash flow."

"What about our reserves in stocks and bonds? Hasn't Linda been stashing away money into a reserve account?" enquired Jason while getting up abruptly as if rejuvenated by his idea.

"Does she know about this cancellation? Did she see the letter?" asked John.

"Yeah, she read it," said Jason.

"What was her reaction? Did you tell her not to tell the others? What the hell did she say?" asked John.

"She said nothing, she just pulled out a cigarette and submersed herself in a nicotine cloud."

"I wished that you hadn't shown that to her. I don't want anything to leak out of this office until we figure out a solution. Jay, go out there and ask her to come in," said John as he began straightening out his tie.

Jason stuck his head out of the door and said, "Linda, can you come in here for a moment please."

She reeked of cigarette smoke, but under the circumstances, reprimanding her for breaking their non-smoking rule when you're standing on the deck of the Titanic just didn't seem appropriate.

"Lin, we're having a little problem here and we were wondering how much money was in the reserve ac......" said Jason.

"You guys spent it," interrupted Linda. "Don't you remember that new graphics computer and software? Well, you are looking at your reserve account."

"Oh, shit," said John rubbing his forehead.

"You boys insisted on getting that system, as a matter of fact you ordered me to have it set up and operational within two weeks of your request. Well, I followed your orders...it was delivered and functioning within a week and a half. You, John, even praised me for my efficiency," said Linda with a smirk on her over confident face.

"Oh, shit," said John.

"Listen, Linda. You take care of the books. Do we have any reserves, any at all, anywhere?" asked Jason, who was now standing in front of her and staring at her with the look of a deer who was caught in someone's headlights.

"If you took what was in the employee's withholding tax money and combined that with the rent money, you'd probably have enough for another two payrolls. Even if you included Flagstaff's last check, we couldn't go beyond two months at the most," said Linda. "It doesn't look good, boys."

"Damn it, Linda, we don't need you to tell us that!" shouted Jason.

"Jay, lay off of her, it's not her fault, it's your fault!" yelled John.

"My fault?" asked Jason while shrugging his shoulders and raising his eyebrows.

"I've been harping on you for the past three years to expand our client base and not to depend solely on Flagstaff, but no...you farted around and blew every other important presentation, including the one that we had today. You had us channel all of our most creative work to the bastards that fucked us today," shouted John while pointing his finger at Jason in an accusatory manner.

"Boys, if you don't mind...this is getting a little too heavy, even for this street-smart gal. I've got a cigarette going back at my desk that is going to give me a lot less grief than you boys are giving me right now. So if you don't mind, I'll be on my way," said Linda while heading for the door.

"Linda," said Jason. "We're not blaming you, please forgive me for my language... things are not..."

Linda just exited the office without acknowledging either one of them, partially butted out her cigarette, put on her coat, and left. Neither Jason nor John knew if she would return. They knew that they would probably not if they were in her position. She didn't return that day.

They called the answering service to take messages while they sat for hours, blaming each other, yelling at each other, crying with each other, until like at the death of a loved one, both realized that the loved one was gone. After coming to this reality, they both sat in silence, still staring at the warm corpse, waiting for the rigor mortise to set in, and contemplating how to announce the death to others. As with the death of a human, some will mourn, others will complacently offer their condolences, while others will relish in the absence of an energetic successful figure.

The parents of the deceased, Jason and John, now reflected on what the impact this death will have on their own lives. Not only themselves but also on those who were dependent on the life blood of the descendant for sustenance. As the tree dies, so do the leaves.

The two of them openly wept as they nervously discussed their fragile personal lives. With two children and a wife, Jason cringed at the thought of going home and announcing that his income was gone.

John, on the other hand, was not married but was supporting a contingency of relatives from his ailing widowed mother, to his handicapped brother, who would probably be either in a nursing home or institutionalized were it not for his financial support.

As the evening hours progressed, Jason went to his office and broke out a bottle of scotch that ironically was presented to him by John on the day that they landed the Flagstaff account. Jason had even forgotten that he had the stash in his filing cabinet until now. They drank and silently stared at each other, like two jilted lovers.

They both knew that those very special creative moments, where their minds met on a pallet of creative colors and ideas, and caressed and fondled each other until orgasmically producing a euphoric outburst of creative pleasure were gone and would never be experienced again. This esoteric climax was almost homosexual in nature with their minds doing the intercourse. It was a feeling that they never discussed but which they both felt with a heated passion and which they now realized would never be experienced again.

As they sat, drank, and silently stared at each other, their minds met one last time, to part as lovers and to part as friends.

CHAPTER 3

To Whom It May Concern,

Seldom have I stared out of this window—especially at three o'-clock in the morning. The silhouette of the pear tree that once bore sweet fruit now stands as a mere skeleton of its former self-casting a moonlit shadow across the table on which I now write this note. The years have transformed its fruit into a mutated form that doesn't resemble a pear at all. Its leaves, once green and healthy, now achieve the color of a yellowed tree passing through a perpetual fall foliage. Even at this time of night, its branches seem to ooze a nectar of despair and sorrow, crying out in pain as it attempts to carry on in spite of its declining years and failed attempts at producing something that is useful and good. As its fruit falls to the ground, no one picks it up. It is left there to rot and decay.

And so I am like that tree. Its decay is my decay, its shadow will disappear as its last branches are cast to the ground to lie in state next to its uneaten fruit. Why have I come to this? Why is my pen shaking as I try to steady my hand? Have I made a wrong decision? Should I have, as I have so often in the past, reasoned my way out of this mental dilemma.

Have I not the courage to do this thing that is the logical end to a sad situation. Has God intervened to stop this act so that another soul will not burn in the eternal fires of hell? Will I not achieve the type of peace that we only dream about and spend money trying to achieve? Is there life after death, and if there is, is it anything similar to the nonsense that we must endure every day of our lives? Is life after death a mere continuum of the crap that we now cope with?

Are our friends there? What about our enemies? Will they torment us for an eternity in some kind of ironic life death cycle? Will we sit in a great room, sip tea while we are bathed in a soothing white light, and have a stimulating conversation with the likes of Aristotle, Benjamin Franklin, and none other than Jesus Himself?

Are these sane questions to ask at three o'clock in the morning? Of course if I were sane I wouldn't be sitting here staring at a decrepit tree and consuming seventy-five generic sleeping tablets and writing this note. Is seventy-five enough? Suppose that they don't work, have I saved the slip, so that I may return them for a full refund? Or should I just buy a name brand and have go at it another night? And now for you, Marnie.

Life is seldom fair, but we accept those things that appear to be inevitable. Acquiescence is not often thought to be noble but is an alternative to confrontation. I am not programmed for failure. I am in debt, my business has failed, I don't have life insurance, I don't have health insurance, creditors are hounding me, my self-esteem is in the toilet. This is not supposed to be happening to me. I've pulled myself through many crisis before, and I've always operated either on or slightly over the line, but this time it's different. I am so far over the line that I don't even know where the line is. Am I crazy? What is it being crazy? Is it like a boundary line in the middle of a forest?

Unless you are viewing the forest from a distance, it is very difficult to determine what side of the boundary you are on. How do you know when you have crossed over from the sane to the insane side? Do bells and whistles go off? Aren't all of the trees the same in the forest? How do you know what tree is the last tree prior to entering the crazy zone? Are there signs, marker, warnings? I haven't seen any, then again everything looks the same from where I am.

My dear family, I have crossed the mental Maginot Line into an abyss of hopelessness and despair. Dante's inferno is pleasurable by comparison. Over the past seven months, I have lost everything, including my self-respect. Those that I thought were dear friends have turned their backs on me. Those that I've given a helping hand to in the past have pulled theirs from me. I have never felt so alone and isolated in all of my life. Because I have owned my own business, my resumes have been discarded by potential employers with the excuse that I might be too independent minded and not a team player. With my money gone and our home on the auction block, this is the only honorable way out for me. I am sorry that I have put you through this, you will all probably hate me for doing this, but I only hope that my resurrection will, if there is such a thing, save my soul from eternal damnation.

Remember that life is a passing breeze through the branches of a tree called forever.

Good-bye,
Jason

One of the empty pill bottles rolled off of the table and bounced as it hit the hardwood floor. He began folding his letter and stuffing it into an envelope. A mound of pills sat next to a full glass of water, his eyes filled with tears as he wrote "Marnie" on the business-sized envelope, licked the flap with his tongue, and pressed it closed.

He grabbed a fist full of pills in one hand and a glass of water in the other and was about to ingest them when he heard feet shuffling toward him from the opposite end of the dark room.

"Stop! Jay, stop right now!" shouted Marnie, who was apparently awakened by the falling bottle and who was now buttoning her flannel house coat as she rushed to him.

She reached for his hand containing the pills that was only inches from his mouth and forcefully lowered it… When she did, the pills fell from his unclenched fist and scattered randomly all over the floor. They bounced like little M & M's, some rolling under the table.

"Jay, I love you...don't do this...don't leave me here alone…"

She then threw herself into his lap, wrapped her arms around his neck, nestled her head under his chin against his quivering chest, and began crying uncontrollably. He gently touched her face that was now awash in tears. He kissed her head, held her tight, and intermittently stared at her delicate features. Until now he hadn't noticed her streaks of gray hairs that glistened in the moonlight. Tears poured from his eyes as he caressed her light brown hair. Their tears mingled as she placed her cheek on his. He knew then that she shared his pain.

They sat in silence, gently swaying for what seemed like an eternity but which in actuality turned out to be only few minutes. As he held her and stroked her head, he thought about the first time that he had met her nineteen years ago.

It was in August at a Harvard College mixer, her long hair was sun bleached, almost blond, her skin was tanned olive brown, and her azure blue eyes reached out and entwined his soul. A low-cut white summer dress clung to the curves of her shapely ninety-pound body. Her rigid posture and slow and graceful movements made her a vision to behold. He knew from that moment on that he had to be with her, know more about her, and show her that he was not only a thinking man but a feeling man as well. She soon reciprocated his feelings, and within six months, they were married.

His parents were vehemently opposed to the timing of the marriage. They were concerned that with only one year remaining in the Harvard Business School MBA program that he would jeopardize his scholarship by marrying.

They also made it clear that although Marnie seemed like a nice person, with just a high school diploma, she was not his mental equal. With Jason's 135 IQ and hyperactive imagination, they were concerned that once they exited from the boudoir he would soon tire of her and find himself extremely unhappy. Just the opposite happened.

The beast in Jason was always calmed by Marnie's placid and simplistic outlook on life. She was again soothing the wild beast tonight. He was her alter ego, her dark and crazy side, her cross to bear. As he held her close, he could smell the apple shampoo in her hair, and the remnants of White Diamonds perfume that she religiously sprayed on every morning.

She lifted her head and stared into his wet eyes. Her tears made her eyes seem even bluer than they were. Her full lips gently and repeatedly kissed his, softly at first and then with an increased intensity. She took his hand and placed it on her breast. Under his hand, he could feel that she was braless as he moved his thumb back and forth across her nipple. She pressed her lips against his and explored his mouth with her tongue.

His other hand slipped between her legs. He pushed her underpants aside and found that her avgina was moist. She breathed heavily while biting his ear lobes and then sticking her tongue into his ear. He unbuttoned her robe and began kissing her breasts while she reached down and undid his belt buckle and then his fly. As she began stroking him and exciting him, he lifted her on to the table and they made love among the sleeping pills and suicide note.

She later fell asleep in his arms on the couch, and he knew that their love making was an affirmation that he must go on. He must do anything to keep them together. He must pull himself out of this depression and find a job, any job.

CHAPTER 4

THE 1952 LINCOLN SPUN ITS TIRES as it tried to move along the muddy road, sinking from side to side like a small sail boat challenging huge ocean swells. The car moved forward as the traction shifted from one back wheel to the other, bouncing up and down as it moved from rut to rut. The dark brown brine came up to the hub caps as the car slowly chugged along. In the wake of the car sprays of brown water, it discolored the white snow that laid on both sides of the muddy road.

It was January and the branches of the trees were heavy with snow and ice as they hung over the road, nearly touching the top of the car. They had passed the last farm house about an hour ago when they turned off of the paved main road and on to this one. It was a mud filled, single lane, pot hole infested, passage through a thick and uninviting forest. He was surprised that his father had brought his brand-new car into this terrain, but it was the setting of their first father and son hunting trip. He had never been away with his dad before, and at eight-years-old, he looked forward to this trip.

A snow covered clearing suddenly appeared on the right of the mud path and the car pulled in and stopped. The man and his son got out and walked for an hour through the cold swampy woods, with snow and water nearly reaching the tops of their boots. The only thing that was taken with them was a double-barreled shot gun that hung by its strap over the father's shoulder. It was 4:30 P.M., and the sun was setting behind the dark forest. It began to snow...slowly at first and then with a ferocity so intense that it became difficult to see twenty feet in front of them.

The father placed his hand on his son's shoulder and stopped him. Thinking that the father had signaled him to go back before the storm intensified, the boy stopped and began backtracking. The sun was now completely out of sight, and it was very difficult to see.

"Sinclair, stop and come here," said the man to his son.

The boy turned around and walked toward his father.

"Son, do you know why we came here?"

"To hunt?" asked the boy while rubbing his gloved hands together as the cold penetrated through the leather into his tiny fingers.

"No," said the man. "We came here to teach you to think and be a man."

"What do you mean, Father?" asked the boy nervously.

"Life is going to be a series of obstacles for you, just as it was for me. You are going to have to learn how to get around those obstacles and survive. Do you understand?" asked the father as he began walking away from the boy.

"Dad, wait for me! Please just slow down a minute," cried out the boy as he began running toward his father, who was already twenty to thirty paces ahead of him.

"Son, you will find your way out of these woods on your own... I am not going to help you... I will be waiting on the main road for you."

The boy began crying, "Daddy, don't leave me here... Please, Daddy, don't leave me!" He could feel the tears freezing on his cheeks as his heart began racing and the snow freezing on his eye lids. The boy then caught his foot on a twig and fell into the snow. He lifted his head and saw his father running from him. As he began to get up, his father fired a shot into the air and yelled at the top of his voice.

"Don't cry, just look at it as a game. You must stay here and slowly count to 200 before moving. If you don't and I see you in my gun site, I may mistake you for a deer and shoot you. Good luck, son," said the father as he disappeared into the dark woods.

It was three days later before the boy emerged from the forest. His feet were nearly frostbitten, his lips and nostrils were crusted with ice, he hadn't eaten in three days, his pants were filled with excrement and urine, and he had a distant and painful look on his face that never left him. Never.

CHAPTER 5

JASON DROVE INTO THE EXPANSIVE PARKING LOT with the want ad that he clipped out of the Boston Globe tucked into his suit jacket pocket. The ad called for "Packers" in the "Fulfillment Center... Immediate Openings." He had absolutely no idea what a packer was, nor did he have any idea what a fulfillment center was. All he knew was that he needed a job, and with 450 resumes out with no responses, he was willing to do most anything.

There were no requirements listed in the ad, and for all intents and purposes, he assumed that it was one of those jobs where if you had a pulse, you were hired. He had many of those types of jobs while working his way through undergraduate school. He did everything from pumping cesspools to baking hot dog rolls in a 102-degree bakery. It had been years since he did any physical labor, but these were not normal circumstances, he told himself as he maneuvered his car into a parking space. He resigned himself to the fact that he must now do anything to survive.

He brought a resume with him but left it on the front seat of his car next to a discarded Hershey Bar wrapper. He thought, "What the hell am I going to need a resume for? It could only hurt me. They'll probably ask me the same crap on an application."

He parked his car next to a ten-year-old Chevy rust bucket. The lot was filled with thousands of what appeared to be seasoned cars. He looked around and didn't see one car that was any newer than four years. Some of them made his car look good. After his BMW and collection of antique cars were repossessed, he purchased this 1983 Cavalier from his brother-in-law. It constantly overheated and used over four quarts of oil a week, but the price was right and it sort of got him where he wanted to go. As he walked toward the building, he noticed the unusual entrances.

The building had two pyramid portals through which hundreds of people were walking. It reminded him of the entrance to the subterranean tunnels in H. G. Well's *Time Machine* where the Enochs lived. They would leave their subterranean caverns at night to snack on fair skinned Elocks. The Elocks would frolic about the country side by day, eating morsels of fattening food left for them by their dinner hosts...the Enochs. This self-serving gesture resulted in a herd of plump Elocks who spent their entire hedonistic existence preparing to become someone's main course. They would then nap outside on the grass and wait for an Enoch to begin munching on them. Not too bright. Then before the sun rose, they would return to their numerous pyramid shaped kiosks that were scattered throughout the countryside, probably talk about their nocturnal culinary delights, and rest for another night of Elock dinning. Jason had always liked this story, and at one point, tried to work it into one of his ad campaigns. The idea didn't even get off of the story board. He imagined that images of Jeffrey Dormer cropping into his client's mind. He was probably right.

Jason was impressed with the size of the building. The structure was so long that its perspective diminished into a small point on the horizon. From what he had read about the place, the building covered thirteen acres and was so large that it had its own ZIP code.

Adjacent to the new and yet uncompleted ultra-modern glass and aluminum structure was an old brick building. It looked like a barnacle on the bow of a new ocean liner.

As he approached the second pyramid portal, he noticed two security guards blocking the entrance. Their short light blue jackets were tucked under a gun in a holster on one side and a long night stick on the other. The two guards stopped him at the glass doors and requested to see his Bigelow of Boston employee identification card. He explained to them that he wasn't an employee, after which he was taken to the security office, where he had to surrender his license for a visitors' pass.

He was then escorted by another security guard to the Human Resource Department. After filling out an employment application, he was taken into a small cubical by a young woman who identified herself as Ms. Hall, Personnel Representative.

As Ms. Hall sat reading Jason's employment application, he very politely asked, "May I ask you a question before we get started?"

Without looking up from the sheet, she said, "Certainly, what is it?"

"I noticed three security cameras in the parking lot near my vehicle, two at the entrance, five in the hallway to the Personnel Department, I mean Human Resource Department, and one on the wall in back of your desk. I was also greeted at the entrance by two armed guards who did everything, except finger print and strip search me. I had to surrender my driver's license just to get in to see you. Let me ask you, is this really a female garment mail order house, or are you working on some sort of secret nuclear weapon?"

Ms. Hall raised her head and smiled politely but was not really amused with his question. She seemed very sensitive to the camera that moved back in forth as it scanned her office.

"Mister…" she hesitated as she checked the employment application. "Mr. Burns, we are the largest mail order house on the East Coast and employ over 2,400 associates. This facility is opened around the clock and fills and ships an average of 47,000 orders a day. Tight security measures are necessary in order to protect our associates."

"Protect them from what, Ms. Hall?" asked Jason.

"Look, Mr. Burns, shall we go on with this interview, or shall we terminate it right now," said Ms. Hall while casually glancing up at the camera that had just moved from side to side on its little metal bracket that was secured to the wall.

"I didn't mean any offense, I was just…'

"Mr. Burns, the position that is available is in our Fulfillment Center on the third shift, and it is that of a Packer," said Ms. Hall, now fidgeting with her mother of pearl glasses that kept sliding down the bridge of her nose.

"Ms. Hall, could you please explain to me what a Fulfillment Center is, and more specifically, what a packer is or does?"

"The job consists of packing garments in boxes for our customers in our warehouse between the hours of 11:00 P.M. to 7:00 A.M. It's a tough shift, but we pay an extra fifteen cents an hour as a night time differential. Your total hourly pay is $6.15."

Jason quickly calculated his weekly pay to be $246. After taxes he would probably take home about $164. It was a far cry from the $500 a day that he had made just seven months ago, but with his savings gone and his home on the auction block, he had no choice. The creditors were relentless.

All day long his family received a constant barrage of harassing telephone calls from credit card companies and banks. His seventeen-year-old daughter seemed to be the most affected by it.

When creditors began coming to the house and leaving nasty notes taped to the front door, she asked a school mate of hers if she could live at her house through her senior year. She told Jason that she could no longer stand the humiliation. Jason reluctantly agreed to the arrangement and told the Swenson's that he would repay them for their troubles just as soon as he was back on his feet. The day that she left, she went into an uncontrollable rage.

She told Jason that he had ruined her life and that she was ashamed at having such a loser as a father. Marnie slapped her across the face in an attempt at stopping her from belittling Jason, but she continued. Each word cut into him like a sharp razor.

She was his first born, and somehow even though he was deeply hurt by her disrespect, he knew that she was right. He silently took her verbal beating in much the same way that a Shiite Muslim takes self-flagellation. He knew that in the silence of his refrain, the verbal abuse represented one of his many penances.

He would never have spoken to his own father in that manner, but his father had never failed his family as he did his. After she left, he poured himself a double bourbon on the rocks and sat gazing at himself in the mirror.

"Well, Mr. Burns, do you want the job or not?" asked Ms. Hall, looking at him impatiently.

"Yes, I do."

"Then you won't mind signing this consent form, which states that you agree to a drug test," said Ms. Hall while sliding a paper across the desk to Jason.

"When should I go for this test?" asked Jason.

"Right after you sign the consent form. The test is done here in our plant by our health nurse," said Ms. Hall while placing a pen on top of the consent form.

"I've got a meeting with my attorney this morning, can I reschedule this test for another day?"

Ms. Hall pointed at the door and said, "If you walk out of that door without having the drug test, you not only forfeit the job, but we will never consider hiring you again for anything under any circumstances, now what shall it be?"

"OK," said Jason as he leaned forward and signed the form.

Ms. Hall picked up the telephone and punched in a three-digit code. "This is Hall from Human Resources, listen, tell Lydia that we have another one for her. I'll tell him that she'll be here to get him in about five minutes."

"Mr. Burns, before you go, I just want to tell you your schedule. Be here tonight at entrance number one at 10:30 P.M. and your supervisor will greet you," said Ms. Hall while placing all of the forms that he filled out into a folder with his name on it. "Follow your instructions explicitly. Remember that you are no different than the other packers. That MBA of yours doesn't mean a thing. As a matter of fact, I almost didn't hire you because of it."

Just then a very matronly-looking nurse came into Hall's room without knocking and asked, "Is he the one?"

"Mr. Burns, this is Mrs. Pacheco, our health consultant. Please go with her and do exactly what she asks," said Ms. Hall.

The nurse walked about ten feet in front of Jason in an apparent attempt at avoiding any small talk. She had his consent form clinched in her hand, and after many twists and turns, went into an area that was identified by a red sign that said "Health Office."

They walked through the outer waiting room that was packed with injured employees and then into the nurse's inner sanctum. A receptionist was talking to patients through a sliding glass window. In back of the receptionist was a long hallway with small patient rooms branching off on both sides. He glanced in every room as they proceeded down the hallway, noticing that each one contained an injured employee. They were also cued up in the waiting room on a triage basis, just waiting for their wounds to be attended to.

After entering the room at the very end of the hallway, he glanced at her badge and said, "Listen, Nurse Pacheco, this is the first time that I have ever had a drug test...what do I have to do?"

"First of all, I am not a nurse... I am a nurse practitioner, second of all, this is not a test where you have to be a rocket scientist to pass...all you have to do is piss into the jar...do you think that you can do that?" said the nurse sarcastically as she went to a stainless steel cabinet above the sink and removed a small sealed kit in a box.

Jason was shocked at her attitude and didn't want to get into argument with her, so he just moved his head up and down to signal his approval. He remembered an old saying that his grandfather frequently used, and which seemed appropriate for the situation, "Never getting into a pissing contest with a skunk."

The small room that they were in contained a toilet, sink, and soap dispenser. The nurse opened the kit, which contained a glass bottle, sticky label, a pair of latex gloves, and a small clear plastic pouch of a blue liquid.

"Now wash your hands," said the nurse while preparing a label with his name on it and pressing it on to the bottle.

"I don't have to tinkle with you in the room, now do I?" asked Jason as he turned on the hot water tap.

"No, I don't get paid to watch people tinkle, but you'll have to do exactly as I say."

As he wiped his hands, the nurse left the room and then quickly came back in. She then removed the toilet tank cover and poured some of the blue liquid into the reservoir. She poured the remainder of the plastic pouch into the water in the toilet. She next tried both faucets that were now not working. Apparently when she left the room, she had shut them off.

"I put the blue stuff into the toilet, so that you couldn't fill the urine jar with toilet water. I also shut the faucets off for the same reason. Now take this jar and give me two ounces of urine. If it's any less than two ounces, I'll give you a second try. If you can't do it, then you can go home and watch cartoons for the rest of your life because you're not working here. Now turn around and put both hands on the sink while I frisk you for any small bottles that may contain your friend's piss."

"You're kidding, right?" asked Jason while still facing her.

"Listen, you either follow procedures, or I'll have to make a note in my report that I think that you are a suspected drug user who refuses to cooperate. Now you know what that means? No job...and a mark against your name. Now what'll it be?" asked the nurse who now put one arm on her hip showing her attitude.

He shook his head in disgust, turned, and put his hands on the corner of the sink. She proceeded to frisk him as though he were a common criminal. Her hands ran up and down his legs, stopping at his crotch where she playfuly humiliated him by rubbing them back and forth twice before removing them.

"Here now fill this up to this mark," said Pacheco, pointing toward a red mark on a plastic jar and then handing it to him.

Without saying a word, he took the jar from her and waited for her to leave. He was not a big one for urinating on command, especially two ounces. He quietly stood there conjuring up thoughts of the Niagara Falls and the white-water rapids of the Colorado River in an attempt at releasing his bodily fluids. Outside of his grunting as he attempted to fill the jar, you could hear a pin drop in the room. Suddenly a strange humming sound came from the ceiling. It sounded like a motor of some sort and came from behind a black translucent ceiling panel. The panel resembled one of those tinted windows that you often see in drug dealers' cars. When he stared up at it, the nose stopped. His concentration once again focused at the task at hand.

He was now thankful for those three cups of coffee that he had before leaving the house. After filling the jar to the two-ounce line, he opened the door to the small cubical and found the nurse waiting in the hallway. She then sealed the jar and told him that if there were any problems with the results that he would be notified before he reported to work that evening. She then called a security guard, who returned his license and escorted him to the first portal and out into the parking lot.

As the guard walked Jason to his car, he raised his hand and scanned the parking lot with a pointed finger and asked, "Tell me something, why are there cameras on each light pole in this lot?"

"It's for your protection," said the guard in a low monotone voice.

"What do you mean? I heard that earlier today, and it just doesn't make any god damned sense. I mean, are there robberies out here, I mean, why are there so many cameras?" asked Jason.

"Listen, Mack, just keep your nose clean and do as you are told and everything will be OK," said the guard while turning around and heading back toward the building.

"What do you mean keep my nose clean?" yelled Jason as the guard moved rapidly away from him without acknowledging his question.

As he put his key into the car door, he glanced up and saw a camera pivot around on its metal bracket and face towards him. It was mounted on a large aluminum light pole that jutted up some twenty feet above him. It was perched like a vulture viewing a dying carcass. Its lens was protruding from the metal box and moved in and out like a turtle with its head bobbing from its shell. It had him in its sights.

As he pulled out of the lot, he rolled down the car window and observed the movement of each camera as he passed the light poles. He looked up and noticed lenses moving outward and their small black boxes moving from left to right, watching him as his car moved toward the parking lot exit.

When he returned at 10:30 that evening, the entire lot was so brilliantly lit that it resembled an airport runway. Straight lines of large aluminum lamp poles stood in perfect alignment. As the powerful halogen lights beamed down, they cast a shadow on black boxes that were perched below them like hungry black crows stalking a fertile corn field. Moving toward the pyramid portal, he noticed that each camera slowly turned its head and followed him. He felt as though he were under a microscope on a Petri dish. He intentionally walked back to the car to see what the cameras would do. Just as he thought, they turned their little bodies and followed him...carefully and slowly moving on their perches.

After entering the building, a security guard gave him a temporary badge and escorted him to the cafeteria where he waited for his supervisor. The hallway leading to the cafeteria was lined with little black boxes. All moving back and forth as associates moved through the hallway.

When they reached the cafeteria, the guard pointed toward a round dinner table and said, "Please wait here. Your supervisor will be out to get you in a short while. Now do not go wondering off. Just stay put."

Jason didn't say a word and merely took a seat as he was instructed. While he was sitting there in the empty cafeteria, he looked at the ceiling and noticed a large black translucent bubble. The florescent lighting on the other side of the bubble highlighted its contents. He could distinctly see three cameras inside of the bubble turn toward him. The noise of their movement was hardly noticeable above the swishing sound of the compressors on the soda machines that were lined up against the wall. His view was suddenly obstructed by a large slender man in his mid-thirties who introduced himself as William Hess.

His blond hair, blue eyes, and rugged Aryan features suddenly fit the name. After explaining the basic rules regarding smoking and taking breaks, the man leaned forward and rested his elbows on the round table, and in an almost inaudible Gregorian tone, said, "Now listen to me carefully. You must follow the entrance and exit routes that have been set up. You must never deviate or invent your own. These routes have been set up for your own safety, and any wondering off on your part could, at best, lead to immediate termination."

"At worst?" asked Jason.

"What?" asked Hess.

"What is the worst that could happen...the worst! You said that immediate termination was the best...then what is the worst that can happen?" shouted

Jason as though he were talking to one of those order walls at a McDonald's drive through...immediately realizing that he should have kept his mouth shut.

Hess's expression changed from indifferent to hostile. "What are you, some wise ass?" asked Hess, whose voice rose in pitch and in tone. "I read your folder over, I know that you're a Harvard big shot. Well, let me tell you something, Burns, that MBA and seventy-five cents wouldn't even get you a cup of coffee in this cafeteria."

"I meant no offense, Mr. Hess, I just..."

Hess stood up like a drill sergeant and put his face an inch away from Jason's and said, "I'm in charge here... Here, you are mine, you do as I say, when I say it. You walk where I tell you to walk. You break when I tell you to break, you go to the shit house when I tell you to. You don't do a god dammed thing unless I tell you. If you got a real big fucking problem with that, just let me know now because the fucking door swings both ways." Hess pointed at the long hallway leading out of the cafeteria and then sat back down. He was like a matador who had just plunged the final blade into a wounded bull. The cameras were moving back and forth as though they were witnessing a feeding frenzy.

"No problem, Mr. Hess, no problem," said Jason while thinking about the shut off notices from the gas, electric, and telephone companies that sat on his bedroom bureau at home. He knew that he should have just sat there and let Hess flex his ego muscles. He bit his lip as he extended his hand for a conciliatory hand shake, which Hess declined. It didn't bother Jason because somehow he knew that he would have declined.

"Let's get to work," said Hess rising and briskly walking toward a hand-made sign that was Scotch taped to the cafeteria wall bearing an arrow that pointed left. Handwritten inside of the arrow was the word "Entrance" that looked like it was done with a heavy felt-tipped pen. As they walked toward a door leading out of the cafeteria, some last-minute workers were about to feed coins into a series of vending machines near the door.

Hess stopped and pointed at his watch and very authoritatively said, "It's not break time yet. Now let's get back to work. Now!" The two black guys mumbled something as they put their change back into their pockets and walked in front of Hess.

Passing through that door into the warehouse was like entering a different world. The ceiling in the cafeteria was nine feet high. The roof in the warehouse was nearly thirteen stories high. Jason's head tilted back as he looked up in amazement. Floor to ceiling shelving contained boxes of what appeared to be garments…a series of tubing ran along the outer wall and contained small moving hooks on which were hung dresses, coats, blouses, and skirts. They moved along on this computerized garment monorail as though they were ghosts cuing up to enter the gates of Hell….moving so quickly that the breeze that they created ruffled Jason's hair. The sleeves of the garments were flapping in an eerie motion that seemed to be beckoning him. Jason had no idea where the garments came from or where they were headed, and Hess had moved so far ahead that any questions that he may have had would have to wait until latter.

The strange thing about the path was that it was marked out in the same type of yellow plastic ribbon that usually marks a crime scene. The yellow tape was attached to long poles that looked like microphone stands. The tape was wrapped around each pole as it continued on its journey. The path that he followed zigged and zagged throughout the warehouse. Jason caught up to Hess and stayed on his heels as they followed the passageway. At one point, it even backtracked and pointed them back in the direction of the cafeteria… In some areas, they actually passed the same spot twice as the pathway continued to twist and turn through the enormous warehouse.

The path took them deeper into the enormous structure. Jason had never been in a building so huge. It reminded him of pictures that he had seen when he was a kid of large airplane hangers that had housed B 52's during the war. He had also seen a video about the Spruce Goose, which was a controversial airplane built by Howard Hughes that was constructed entirely of spruce. It was only piloted once, by Hughes himself, and was then hidden in a large hanger with around the clock security to keep the curious away. As he quickly glanced around the warehouse, he thought that this space seemed even larger to him than that.

Every so often, there was a break in the yellow tape. It was here that other associates entered or exited the path, much like a clover leaf in a super highway. It was at one of these openings that Hess exited and walked toward a long open isle with small cubicles bordering both sides for as far as you could see.

Hess turned around and said, "These are packing stations. I will assign a lead person to train you, after which you will be assigned your own packing station. Your trainer will be here shortly. She's been with us for five months and is the fastest packer on this shift. I wish that I had ten more like her."

Hess walked down the long corridor, randomly poking his head into different cubicles and yelling at its occupants. Jason couldn't make out the jest of the confrontation, but one of the packers grabbed all of the garments that were in her area and threw them at Hess while shouting, "You fucking asshole. You can't talk to me like that... I'm going as fast as I can...you're never satisfied... I... I'm trying my best..."

He then picked an armful of the garments that were strewn in the corridor outside of her cubical and threw them back at her and said, "You're fired...now get your ass out of here!"

He walked briskly down the aisle past the other cubicles toward his desk that sat at the end of the long thoroughfare.

The woman exited her cubical and ran towards him, tears streaming down her cheeks, and pleaded, "Mr. Hess, I'm sorry...please forgive me... I need this job...I've got three kids...please give me a chance... I lost my cool."

Hess swung around on his heels, pointed his finger into the air at what was probably where the exit was behind the walls of garments, and said, "I want you out of here. Now get your stuff and leave!"

Jason was observing this scene from the other end of the corridor as though he was watching a Fellini movie. Just then two security guards appeared out of nowhere and got on both sides of her and gingerly escorted her down the yellow taped path. The intensity of her profanity diminished as she apparently moved farther from him. As he stood there waiting for his trainer, he glanced up toward the ceiling and saw a black translucent bubble mounted on a metal crossbeam midpoint on the ceiling, This explained the rapidity of the security guards' response, he thought after the incident.

As he stood there looking up, a familiar voice in back of him said, "Hello, I am your trainer."

Turning around quickly, he could feel his heart beating faster and the blood rushing to his head. When he made eye contact, he couldn't believe this strange and humiliating coincidence.

"Linda, how are you.?"

His former secretary looked at him as a hunter does when a doe appears in his gun site. Her finger was on the trigger, and she knew it.

"Well, I'll be damned, it's Jason Burns," said Linda as she moved her head up and down with a cocky smirk on her face.

"Linda, I don't know if I can do this.. " said Jason while looking over his shoulder to see if Hess was in the vicinity.

"I can't believe that I've got Mr. Harvard, Mr. Creativity, Mr. Failure right here reporting to me. Me, a high school drop-out," she laughed while slapping her thigh.

"You know that after you closed the office, my husband left me. I couldn't find a job at my age, and we couldn't live the way we were living on Harvey's pay, so we lost our home. Harvey blamed me. He said that I was crazy for sticking with you for so many years. He said that I should have been able to see the handwriting on the wall. You know something, Jay, Harvey was right," said Linda as she began walking toward one of the vacant cubicles with Jay at her side.

"Linda, I'm sorry," said Jason as he stepped up into the cubical in back of Linda.

She smiled at him and said, "Jay, whatever goes around, comes around. It gives me great pleasure to see you here. You must have hit bottom, or you wouldn't be working in this hell hole at two o'clock in the morning for six bucks an hour. You ruined my life, and I'll never forgive you for it."

After seven months of relentless interviews, over 400 resumes, and scorn from his family and friends, his decision to take this job was admitting to himself that he had struck bottom. He thought that he could discretely work from eleven to seven, take home a pittance of a salary, and try and get himself back into the mainstream during the day. He would work like Rumpelstiltskin, weaving all night in the quiet and solitude of his obscure purgatory and then when the sun rose, so would he. He would emerge in the morning, silent about his nocturnal travails, get a few hours of sleep, and start a new batch of resumes. If asked why he looked so tired, he fabricated some lie about either insomnia or nightmares.

Having Linda as his superior plunged him to a new mental low. She was still yelling at him, but he blocked out her insane rhetoric and arm waving. He stared at her moving lips, that in his mind, were now disconnected from the vile words that were passing threw them. She was probably right in feeling the way that she did, but who shared his pain? Certainly not her. As her words became audible again he suddenly had the impulse to wrap his hands around her throat and squeeze her neck until her words stopped.

"You crazy bitch, is this the way that you train new packers?" shouted Hess with a grin on his face. He had been eavesdropping and apparently approved of Linda's nasty outburst.

In a convoluted way, Jason somehow welcomed Hess's intervention. He thought that it probably prevented him from committing a homicide.

As Hess walked away he shouted over his shoulder, "Give'em hell, Lin."

She then spent the next seven minutes showing him how to pack garments into a box, tape it, place a label on it, and throw it on a moving conveyor belt next to the cubical.

"You think that you got this?" she asked as she began moving toward the cubical opening toward the corridor.

"I'm all set," he said. He was going to say that a lobotomized chimpanzee could probably learn and perform this task faster and more accurately than any of the 135 or so packers working the graveyard shift, including her, a seasoned and experienced packer. But he refrained.

"Under no circumstances are you to leave this cubical once the shift begins." She leaned over and whispered into Jason's ear, "There is a camera in each cubical watching your every move. Don't look now. but it's mounted on the tubing holding the florescent light just above your head."

He couldn't understand the sudden change in her attitude, but any small talk aside from being the recipient of her yelling and condescending was a welcomed change. Maybe she just got these feelings off of her chest and was now ready to resume some kind of civil working relationship. Who knows, he thought to himself.

Her eyes moved upward as if to signal the camera's location.

"I've got to go and do my own work now. Any questions?"

"Linda, what's with the yellow tape and winding pathway? Are we in Oz? I mean what's going on?" asked Jason quickly with a perplexed look on his face.

"Listen, I've got to go... I can't answer any more questions," said Linda nervously while trying to ignore the tiny humming black box.

Suddenly out of nowhere, two security guards in light blue uniforms appeared at the entrance to the cubical. A burly guard whose buttons on his shirt were nearly popping open from his muscular chest said, "Linda, can we talk to you for a minute?"

Linda's eyes shifted from side to side as she moved forward. She placed her hand in Jason's and squeezed it. Without saying a word, she followed them in the forest of garments at the end of the hallway and disappeared. Jason never saw her again. He latter naively assumed that she had transferred to another shift.

Remembering what Linda said, he worked as fast as he could but kept looking at his watches. His bladder was nearly exploding as the one o'clock break signal sounded. He left his cubical and proceeded toward the pathway he had entered this sector on, but it was gone. He then sheepishly followed a man carrying a small plastic Igloo cooler who looked as though he were headed for the cafeteria. The man entered another pathway, and Jason followed.

As they walked along, Jason asked the man, "What happened to the other pathway?"

The man turned and said, "Oh, they change them all of the time. Don't ask me why, but they do."

This new path wound in and out of rows of garments. Jason, at one point in order to proceed, had to push some aside, as he would protruding branches in a forest. This path also had yellow plastic tape on both sides marking the way as does a guard rail on a highway. More and more people entered the slow and congested cue. It reminded him of the gridlock on the Southeast Expressway. It took nearly ten minutes to reach the cafeteria, which used up almost all of the fifteen-minute break.

Jason sat alone sipping a diet soda and reading a paper back. He looked up and noticed that most of the employees on break were staring at him as though he were an extraterrestrial who was holding some sort of alien object in his hands.

He also felt the piercing eyes of an inanimate object above him. The cameras in the overhead black bubble were all turned toward him in an obvious attempt at viewing his reading material. Nothing in Jason's totally unstructured life had prepared him for this. He pulled his book closer to his body in an attempt at removing it from the prying lenses.

At the conclusion of the break, he walked to the door through which he came but found it locked. As he looked through the glass door, he saw that that pathway was gone. He turned around and noticed employees going through another door at the opposite end of the cafeteria. During the short break, someone had set up a new maze. All of the yellow tape had been rearranged into a new labyrinth, with new obstacles, that the employees unquestioningly followed until they arrived at the work site.

At seven in the morning, an electronic screech filled the air, signaling the end of the shift. The employees then followed yet a new maze to the time clock section of the plant. The previous path had been erased as though it had never existed. As he walked along, he periodically glanced up and noticed more black boxes that were mounted on steel cross beams about fifteen feet above him, a ll humming away as they watched the herd moving below.

A cadre of security guard stopped and frisked every employee before exiting the plant. Some of the women complained as searching hands moved inappropriately in and out of the more predominant nooks and crannies of their anatomies. In front of him, a young woman was being groped at inappropriately in search of hidden garments. His first impulse was to pull her away and demand an apology, but she stood there taking it, and they stood there giving it, and in a convoluted way, his interference somehow seemed more inappropriate than the process that was taking place. He merely turned away and waited for his moment of humiliation.

This place is like Auschwitz without the gas chambers, he thought as two guards ran their hands over his body while he held his jacket above his head as they had instructed.

Before leaving the parking lot, he sat there for a while starring catatonically through the steamed windshield of his car as the sun rose slowly above the horizon. He then closed his eyes, and in a moment of self-pity, reviewed the debilitating events of the evening.

My life has become a chaotic compilation of disjointed seconds, he thought as he rubbed his head that was now throbbing with pain. "I wish I were dead."

CHAPTER 6

HE SWUNG BACK AND FORTH in the white cushioned wicker chair that hung suspended from the porch ceiling by large pieces of braided hemp. A warm ocean scented summer breeze filled his lungs as he slowly moved back and forth like a pendulum in a grandfather clock. He remembered that last year at nine-years-old, he could hardly reach the swing without a boost from his mom, but over the past year, he had grown about four inches and exercised his new independence by getting in and out of it unassisted.

The setting sun was shining through the tops of the waves as they broke onto the pebble less beach about a hundred feet in from of the porch. Each wave made a crashing sound that mesmerized him as he watched the sky change from blue to a palate of colors from cobalt red to soft violet. His father's new 1954 Lincoln sat in the driveway next to the house. The driveway was completely white and was made up of crushed powered sea shells. Of all of the property that his parents owned, this was his favorite. Not only for its proximity to the ocean and pristine setting at the end of a peninsula but because this was a sanctuary. Here the craziness was put on hold; here in this demilitarized zone, the unwritten rules said that there shall be peace. Here there shall be no arguments and fits of temper. Here there were only civil words and civil actions. Here, though only for a month a year, was a place that he thought about for eleven months.

His mom in her summer dress was on her hands and knees in the sand dune near the front of the porch planting beach plumbs. His father sat in the stationery wicker chair on the other end of the porch reading the New York Times and smoking his pipe.

His father put down the paper and walked up to him and said, "Let's go and check the lobster traps. If we're lucky, we will be eating lobster tonight."

The boy continued to swing as though nothing had been said and his father were not there.

His father stopped the swing, bent over, and said, "Come, Sinclair, let's go before it gets dark."

His mother stepped on to the porch, and while brushing her long brown hair back, said, "Go with your father, I'm just dying for a good lobster dinner. There must be something in the traps, it's been two days since they've been baited."

The boy still did not move or acknowledge that he was being spoken to.

His mother bent over and kissed him on the forehead and quietly said, "Please go with your dad."

It was the way that she said it that made him get up and begin walking toward the boat with his father. The tone of her voice implied that if he did not go with his father that his father might suddenly decide to change the rules. He knew that the rules at this peaceful haven must not be changed, and the thought that he might be responsible, even though indirectly, for changing them filled him with guilt.

He sat on the small bow seat as his father shoved off and then jumped into the boat. He was wearing blue Bermuda shorts and sneakers, his father had on white slacks, madras shirt, and sandals. The oars gently touched the waves as his father grunted from the strain while they moved farther and farther out toward a red marker that bounced up and down in the small ocean swells. The red buoyant plastic ball splashing in the murky ocean brine marked the spot where one of the lobster traps was located.

His father pulled in the oars, reached over the side of the bobbing boat, grabbed the red marker, and pulled in the rope that was attached to it. At the end of the rope was a wooden lobster trap with what appeared to be two three-pound lobsters in it. His father removed them from the trap, placed them in a large rope tied burlap bag, threw the trap overboard, and began rowing again. Their destination was a blue maker about twenty feet from them.

His father stopped the boat about ten feet from the second marker and pulled the oars in and said, "Son, it is because I care about you that I conduct these tests. As my son, you have a tremendous responsibility. You must be stronger that the rest so that you can overcome any obstacle and lead us into the future. You will acquiesce to no one, you will follow no one. I will prepare you for the ultimate challenge..."

Just then he reached over to a very frightened sobbing young man, grabbed him by the arm, and with one quick motion, tossed him overboard. His small body disappeared under the dark ocean but popped up again with his arms flapping. Without a life preserver, it was very difficult for him to stay afloat. He began swimming toward the boat, but it moved quickly away from him as his father rowed faster and faster.

"Good luck, Sinclair, I'll be waiting for you on shore."

The little boy began swimming frantically but was soon sinking. His mouth gulped in large amounts of cold salty water as he rapidly moved his arms to stay afloat. He looked toward the beach but could barely see the large white summer house. The house was now a bath in pastel colors that were reflected from the colorful sunset. He could also barely see his father's boat that continued to move away from him. The water took on a coldness as the sun sank into the ocean. The coldness penetrated every joint in his body as he placed one arm in front of the other, not looking up, not even aware as to whether he was heading in the right direction. He felt cramps in both of his legs but would not surrender to the will of Neptune.

He didn't know how he did it, but he could feel his feet touch the bottom. As he walked toward the beach with the water touching his chin, he could see silhouettes of his father striking his mother and she falling onto the wet sand. He knew that he would never return to this place. Never.

CHAPTER 7

Jason checked both watches as he sat at the kitchen table. It was 10:30 P.M., and he knew that in about ten minutes he would have to leave for work. Something that he equated with a prostitute hitting the streets. Except that in his case, he wasn't an expensive call girl. At $6.00 an hour, he compared himself with a whore. Not only a whore, a cheap whore.

He then began moving his finger slowly in concentric circles around the rim of a cup of dark coffee that sat in front of him. Dark circles surrounded his eyes and his face was sunken in. He had lost nearly thirty-five pounds in the last ninety days, but more importantly, he lost his dignity and self-respect.

Trying to survive on two hours of sleep a night had taken its toll. He looked bad and felt bad. At forty-eight-years-old, he looked at himself as a destroyed man. Even though he tried talking upbeat to his wife and kids, telling them that everything was going to turn around, he knew that he was lying, but much worse…they knew that he was lying. He thought and moved lethargically with no forethought, his passion was gone.

The intensity of bazaar occurrences at Bigelow's had increased geometrically over the past three months, along with the number of security guards and cameras. Last week Ray, a Viet Nam vet who worked in the cubical in front of him, was found in a pool of blood in the men's room with both of his wrists slashed. He was the only person that ventured over to Jason's table during the 4:00 A.M. lunch break and shared conversations with him. Jason would sit and take notes as Ray rambled on, sometimes paranoically, about what he thought was going on.

"I spent twenty-five years in intelligence, and I know a fucking skunk when I smell one," Ray would say.

"There's something going on here, and it's not healthy. I've been following them pricks around for the last two weeks after I punched out, and they all seem to end up in that fucking brick house. I tried to peek into one of their windows but was caught by one of them Gestapo assholes. A mean bastard at that, even by my standards."

Ray would then wipe his forehead, run his hand across his gray crew cut that seemed to stand at attention, and completely change the subject. Time and time again, Ray's conversations would switch gears into an entirely different topic without skipping a heartbeat. Jason wondered if Ray did it intentionally, suspecting that the cameras may also have an audio capability, or perhaps he was just plain crazy. He never really talked about what he did in "Nam," as Ray called it...but he seemed to indicate that it had something to do with counter intelligence.

To people sitting close to Ray, he seemed to be a couple of logs short of a full cord, but to Jason, his stories were lucid and interesting.

During one of their conversations, Ray asked Jason for his pen and a piece of paper. Jason ripped a sheet out of his note book and slid it and the paper across the table.

While writing Ray told Jason, "Just keep on talking, I'm listening...go ahead... I can hear you."

Ray shielded the paper with his arm as Jason talked about something totally unrelated. It didn't matter because he knew that Ray wasn't listening...but he continued anyway.

When he finished his note, Ray looked up, winked at Jason, ran his hand over his crew cut, and smiled at the cameras that were now stretching their little necks trying to catch a glimpse at what he wrote.

He then sporadically jumped onto the chair like a mad man and held his note in both hands above his head. The note said, "Fuck you." He then blew a kiss to the black bubble while laughing and waving. The expression on his face resembled Shemp from the Three Stooges. Everyone in the immediate vicinity put down their sandwiches and soft drinks and just gazed at him in utter disbelief. They didn't know whether to laugh, applaud, or just continue to sit there in total shock.

The cameras' necks then moved quickly back into their boxes like little frightened snails. Just then the lunch siren sounded, and Jason shook his head while smiling at Ray and said, "Saved by the bell."

Jason liked Ray, even though many of his stories seemed a little disconnected. He attributed Ray's short attention span to probably some unspeakable war experience. Maybe it was Agent Orange, or maybe the war had nothing to do with it at all. Since no one knew him, maybe everyone used the war as an excuse for him. Maybe there was no excuse at all. Regardless Jason liked him and found him to be a loyal newfound friend.

His death came as a shock to him. What little personal information he did share with Jason seemed to indicate that he was happy with his life and with the military disability pension that he was collecting monthly. Outside of a little arson problem that he was trying to work out with his son and the local police in his town he spoke of his family with great love and respect. His death didn't make any sense to Jason, nor to any of his co-workers. It really bothered him.

The worker who found Ray told Jason that he had written something in blood on the men's room wall before he died. He couldn't make out what it said, but part of the cryptic message was an arrow drawn in blood. The arrow pointed up toward the ceiling. One of the other employees said that perhaps Ray was pointing toward God as an act of contrition or forgiveness before he died.

Jason knew that that wasn't true because Ray had told him that since the war, he had become an avid atheist. Even at his funeral, all religious symbols were conspicuously absent.

The men's room was sealed off for two days while what appeared to be forensic people were seen going in and out with their little black bags. When the room was finally opened to the workers again, Jason was the first to go in with the person who found him.

He showed Jason approximately where Ray's body was found and also where the blood smeared arrow was drawn on the wall. The entire bathroom had been steamed clean, but Jason visualized how the arrow might have appeared. It was pointing up toward a translucent black ceiling tile. Jason knew what it was, but he had never seen one in that men's room before.

At Ray's wake, a picture of a thirty-year-old Marine in full dress uniform sat on his flag draped casket. The looks on the faces of his family reflected disbelief and not grief. They knew, as so did Jason, that Ray would never have taken his own life.

His wife whispered to Jason as he paid his condolences, "There lies a man who fought his way out of a jungle with a jammed rifle and a knife just so that he could come home to his family. Jason, he was your friend, on Ray's soul, you must find out who did this thing." She pointed at the casket and said, "Ray will never rest in peace until you do."

Jason was visibly shaken by what she said, gave her a hug, and briskly walked out of the front door.

That night he sat alone during the 4:00 A.M. lunch break and jotted his feelings and observations into his log book. The log was a journal of all the incidents that occurred at Bigelows since he began working there. In the last ninety days, he had compiled nearly a hundred pages of information. Dates, times, names, injuries, and personal observations filled his diary. Ray was the only Bigelow person that he shared his log with. Many of the entries were incidents that Ray had experienced.

"Man, you are crazier than a shit house rat," Ray told him when he began his journal. "That thing is going to get your ass into a pile of donkey dung."

But as time progressed and more and more bizarre incidents occurred, and Ray's attitude changed. He viewed Jason and his journal as a chronicler scribe who would document these events and maybe one day appear on *20/20*.

He once told Jason, "I can see myself talking to Mike Walace in my full-dress uniform...spiffy... I'll even give you a few words...after all you did go to fucking college."

About two weeks before Ray died, a new female employee joined them at their table in the cafeteria one evening. As they sat there talking, blood suddenly began dripping out of both of her ears and down her cheeks. She reached up and touched the red warm substance that oozed out of her earlobes and inadvertently smeared it over her face and hands. She panicked and ran screaming out of the cafeteria. She didn't return, and that was the last night that they saw her.

A week later, Ray's right ear began bleeding profusely, but he said that it probably had something to do with the war. Jason questioned him about the location that he worked the night before, but he just ignored him.

"Maybe there's something in that new building that you were working in last night that did this," Jason stated.

"What's in there? A big space gun? Yeah, maybe there's aliens in there that like to feed on ear wax...they just love the stuff...they're only tiny little bastards that jump up into your fucking ear lobe and just eat that wax until they finally let go and fall out onto the floor...burping and slurping ear wax."

"Ray, I'm serious...they could be using something in there that is causing this problem, and I don't mean space people," Jason said with a serious look on his face.

"You just listen, little buddy, I'll find out what caused my fucking ears to have a period...and if it is little space bastards... I'll pick them up and chew their little green heads off," said Ray while putting his clenched fist up to his mouth and twisting it.

He continued to dab each ear with a long piece of toilet paper that he removed from his pocket. As they talked, blood seemed to coagulate and the bleeding subsided.

Ray did tell him that he had never suffered any symptoms like that in the seventeen years since his discharge. He also had a way of covering up his fears and anxieties with humor...or at least what he thought was humor. Most of his humor referred to private body parts or disgusting bodily functions. All of his physical aches and pains, which were many, he attributed to the war. Strangely enough his ear continued to bleed until he died. That evening the cameras seemed particularly interested in his ears. They kept panning in and out as if they were performing some sort of a medical procedure.

To prove to Ray that someone behind those cameras had singled the two of them out as a potential trouble makers while at lunch, he tore a page out of his log and threw it into the trash barrel. He then stood behind a poll with Ray and within two minutes watched two security guards come into the cafeteria, go through the garbage in the barrel, and walk away with his page.

As he sat at the kitchen table, he felt more depressed as he thought about Ray. No one from Bigelow's, outside of himself, went to his funeral. It was really sad. His flag draped casket sat at the end of a long room with lines of military personnel walking briskly by and saluting his picture.

It had been a month since Ray's death, but as he sat there drinking his coffee and staring into space, it seemed to him as though it were only yesterday. This evening every cell in Jason's body rebelled against going into work, but he dragged himself away from the table, put on his coat, and began his sojourn to hell. The twenty-minute ride seemed to pass quickly this evening, the traffic on the highway seemed unusually light, but as he approached the exit, he could see the line of bright red tail lights that seemed to wrap around the clover leaf.

He came to a complete stop in back of a Jeep that still had its amber right blinker light still on and thought that perhaps there might have been an accident. As he edged slowly off of the highway, he couldn't see any activity up ahead that would indicate that a traffic mishap had occurred. The bumper to bumper traffic continued all of the way to Bigelow's. He kept glancing at his watches as he nervously moved his foot from gas to brake and back. He also kept moving his eyes to the temperature gauge. The indicator was moving toward the red danger zone when he finally pulled into the parking lot. He was fifteen minutes late.

From his vantage point, which was about a sixteenth of a mile from the huge building, he could see the blue, white, and red lights reflecting off of the building. He was cut off by an ambulance with its siren blasting as it raced out of the parking lot. Through its back window, he noticed two EMT's bent over a woman on a stretcher holding some sort of plastic device over her face.

He parked his car and approached the building. The entire drive way in front of the building was filled with police cars, ambulances, and fire trucks, all with their motors running and lights blinking. The front door was held open by two Bigelow's security guards as a steady stream of medical, police, and fire personnel pushed gurneys with bodies strapped to them out into the waiting cold. It had snowed that afternoon, and a few of the gurneys stopped short once they reached the snow encrusted sidewalk. Attendants on both sides pushed them over the snow clumps towards the waiting ambulances. Each then reaching down and collapsing the telescopic metal poles and gently lifting the gurney into the vehicle and then closing the two swinging back doors. The ambulance then sped away, fish tailing, sirens blaring through the poorly plowed parking lot.

As one ambulance pulled away, another drove up to take its place. A cue of gurneys waited inside for the next ambulance. When Jason approached the glass front doors, he noticed coughing and vomiting employees on gurneys as far as the eye could see, all being attended to by one frazzled EMT.

He approached one of the security guards who was rigidly standing near the front door. He looked like a member of the Royal Army guarding Buckingham Palace.

"Say, what the hell is going on here?" asked Jason while fidgeting with his bar-coded employee badge, anticipating the guard's next question.

"You can't go in there," said the guard while opening the glass door for a gurney.

Jason flashed his badge and move forward toward the opened door. The security guard grabbed his arm and said, "I said that you can't go in there. Can't you see that we've got a god damned problem here?"

The guard said, "All employees are to meet in the Winslow building."

"I'm sorry, we're supposed to meet where?" asked Jason while backing up and making room for another gurney to pass.

"The Winslow building," said the guard while pointing at the brick building that was attached to the warehouse. He now knew the name of that strange brick building, he thought as he walked toward the right, barely avoiding a collision with yet another gurney. As he approached, he could see other employees silently filing through the front entrance. Since no one had any information, there was little talk going on.

As he entered the white columned portico into a large hall, he noticed oil paintings of a man, that with the exception of the brown hair, seemed to resemble Mark Twain. He also noticed a glass display case hanging on the wall that contained some company artifacts. Jason made his way through the crowd to get a closer look. The case contained an assorted collection of small packets, each with the imprint "Bigelow Seed Company." Also in the case was an old yellow catalogue with the printing, "Bigelow 1894 Spring Planting Catalogue."

Apparently the Bigelow Company was a lot older than he had originally thought. Somewhere along the way, one of the Bigelows had made the transition from 19th to 20th century and plugged into the lucrative "shop by mail the cities are too violent" business.

"Can I have your attention please!" blared a voice from the right side of the hall.

He turned around and saw Hess standing with a bull horn. Around him were at least 500 people.

"We've had a little mishap here tonight, and a few of our associates have been taken to area hospitals as a precautionary measure."

"A few employees?" Jason mumbled to the woman standing next to him. "I counted at least forty people in the hall way. Not to mention the others that were taken away before I got here. What the hell is he talking about...a few."

The woman put her lips next to his ear and said, "The fucking lying bastards."

This kind of language coming out of the mouth of a meek-looking grayed haired middle-aged woman really threw Jason off at first, but over the last ninety days, he had come to accept it as commonplace. At first he felt extremely uncomfortable with these people but soon discovered that even though they were uneducated and inarticulate, it had nothing to do with their basic values. They were good people with lousy vocabularies and little or no knowledge about the world outside of what affected them personally. As he studied them and logged some of their behavior into his journal, he sort of felt like Margarete Meade. He did this more to try and understand how they could be so complacent to the kind of atmosphere that someone at Bigelow's intentionally created for them. He certainly was not a social anthropologist, but he felt that some force in this factory was manipulating them and taking advantage of their simple nature.

"Please, folks, can I have your attention," yelled Hess through the bull horn again. "Once again I would like to say that no one has been hurt. The problem, as we understand it, can be traced to new plastic office chairs that were brought into the second floor yesterday. The smell of the new plastic got into the heating ducts and caused some people to get light headed. The problem is being corrected as I speak, and you are all to return to work tomorrow night."

A black teenager standing near Jason yelled out, "Heh, Hess, your fucking nose is growing."

The crowd applauded spontaneously and shouted cat calls at Hess, who attempted to appear unflappable. Hess probably would have fired him had he not been standing in the midst of a crowd of 500 cheering people who thought that the kid was right on target. Instead he walked out of the side emergency exit and into the night. The crowd let out a brief nervous laugh and then began exiting the hall. Jason couldn't believe that they had bought Hess's story.

He caught up to the black kid and asked, "You don't really believe that son of a bitch, do you? I mean molded plastic doesn't put people in hospitals. You don't have to be a Rhodes Scholar to know that. Would you be willing to help me get to the bottom of this?"

"Listen, professor, I seen you around here, and you ain't one of us. You're probably one of them. I ain't putting my fucking ass on the line for nobody...specially for some asshole who walks around with a fucking library tucked in his jacket," said the kid as he picked up his pace in the parking lot and strutted towards his car. "My friend Tyrone disappeared from the face of the fucking earth last summer. You think I'm going to end up like him. I don't fucking think so."

"Listen, I want to help... I don't even know who they are...so how could I be one of them? I'm a guy like you, out of work and packing crap in little boxes until something better comes along," said Jason catching up to the kid.

The cold winter air whipped across the parking lot and blew the kid's hood down, which he quickly pulled back up. The parking lot was illuminated by a full moon that had a white snow ring around it. Any decent New Englander knew that that meant more snow was on its way.

The kid stopped and pointed up at one of the cameras that was mounted on the parking lot light pole and said, "Go ahead, tell the man that you are after him...go ahead! Tell 'em! You'll end up like fucking Tyrone."

"Listen, kid."

"My name is TJ."

"My name is Jason."

"What happened to Tyronne?" asked Jason as he motioned TJ to walk to his car where they could sit and talk out of the cold."

"He was an asshole like you. Snoopin' around, tryin to git the truth... you know what it got 'em? A one-way ticket to nowhere...and that's where you're goin..."

"I don't understand," said Jason as they walked to a dark part of the parking lot after realizing that TJ had no intentions of sitting in his car.

"One day he just doesn't show up for work. I called his house and got no answer...figured that he was probably with some chick...well, one day turns into three, so I goes to his house to check out the situation. Knock on the fucking door until guy next door comes out in his fucking jockey shorts. He tells me to get my ass out of there before he kicks it real good. So I says, listen, chump, my friend lives here. He says not any longer...moved out last night...couple of white dudes moved his stuff about midnight."

"Was it Tyrone and the white dudes?" asked Jason.

"No, it was just the white dudes. No fucking Tyrone. That's the strange part...man...if I was movin' ...first, I would be there myself...second, I wouldn't trust no white dudes to clean out my crib...and I know that Tyrone wouldn't either," said TJ as he fixed his hood, so that it cast a shadow on his face, thus obscuring it from the cameras. "Listen, man, I gota go... I shouln't have opened my big fucking mouth...see ya," said TJ as he opened his car door, started the engine, and began scraping the frost off his windshield.

Jason noticed a black van with no markings pull out from the side of the building and park near the exit with its engine running and parking lights on. By the time that he started his own car, TJ was driving out of the lot. The black van then put on its low beams and rapidly followed TJ out of the lot and on to the highway.

Jason's first impulse was to follow them, but he thought about what his late friend Ray had told him, "Jay, you're crazier than a shit house rat." Maybe things were getting on his nerves, maybe his imagination was running amuck. Maybe Ray was right.

He didn't think about the incident until the following night when he heard the report about TJ's accident. An eyewitness account had stated that he saw a black van push TJ's car into a ravine. His car exploded. What was left of TJ was buried that Saturday.

CHAPTER 8

THE FREEZING SLEET PELTED HIS FACE and blew the plastic yellow hood off his head; his cheeks felt as though thousands of pins were being inserted at the same time, his tiny body shivered as the front of the rain slicker flapped open and close. He clung onto his books as though he were holding sacred and holy religious scrolls. He tucked them under his arm in an effort at protecting them from the downpour, which ran in and out of the many folds and crevices in his rain slicker. It looked like a river running through a great yellow terrain.

With his free hand, he reached and pulled the hood back onto his head that was now dripping with a combination of water and ice. His ears were so cold that he dared not touch them for fear that they may break off and fall to the ground. He would then have to attend classes tomorrow looking like Vincent Van Gough. Standing next to him were two of his class mates; they, too, were soaked and wet like two little river rats. They were kidding him about his rain slicker and told him that he looked like an old Glouster fisherman. He was used to their remarks, which seemed to go on without end. The three years that he had attended public school were filled with ridicule and insults.

He couldn't understand why his father had removed him from private school and put him in this public school in the worst part of town. He knew that they had the money, so it wasn't a matter of finances. With the exception of these two, he had made no friends. He often thought, why would he consider these two friends...they were relentless in their verbal and physical whip lashing. A cacophony of words didn't deter him from clinging to their abuse...like the proverbial abused child who clings to its oppressor. He knew that they were using him, stealing his allowance money, stealing his lunches, and borrowing but not returning personal items, such as his gold watch. He knew the cruel truth that no other kids in his school would bother with him.

The first day that he came to school, these sons and daughter of blue-collar workers greeted him with a beating so severe that he couldn't open his right eye for a week. His father seemed almost pleased when he saw him that night, his face covered with blood and his eye completely closed.

After six months, they at least stopped screaming vulgar remarks when the limousine pulled up and a fully uniformed chauffeur got out and opened the back door for him. Many of these kids had only seen a limousine like this at funerals or weddings. He felt badly for Chauncey the chauffer. He felt that the remarks yelled at him would hurt Chauncey's feelings and maybe provoke him to quit. He felt that if he quit, no one would wipe away his tears, share a sandwich with him in the servants' quarters while he shared the day's events with him. He would have no one to give him a hug when he felt as though he were a ship wrecked survivor in a sea of sharks. Even though Chauncey had no family of his own, he felt as though he were his son, and he knew that Chauncey felt the same way.

Just as his hood blew off for the third time, he looked up and saw the big black Lincoln Continental limo. His father traded the family limo in every year and got a new one. He liked this one better than last year's model. This new 1954 model had real styling he thought as the limo came to a sudden stop with Chauncy leaping out while the car was still rocking.

"Chauncey, these are my friends and they will be coming home with me to play," he said as he looked sideways at the two chubby little wet rodents.

Chauncy walked over and said, "Master Sinclair, you know that you cannot bring your friends home, it is forbidden."

The frozen rain seemed to intensify, blowing in sheets, nearly knocking Chauncey's black chauffeur's hat from his head. The rest of his uniform was now saturated with cold water, and his body became frigid. He stared first at the little boy and then to his friends, and without saying a word...opened the back door to the limo and signaled for them to enter.

The three little dripping gnomes ran into the car, closed the door, and huddled together like tad poles in a lily pond. The back of the limo was spacious and contained its own radio, which the three immediately turned on. A love song was just finishing on their favorite radio station, 91.3, so they knew that a fast one was soon to follow. The radio announcer's voice echoed as though he were standing inside of a fifty-gallon drum.

"And now all of you cats out there, the number one song You Ain't Nothing but A Hound Dog!" yelled the announcer as his voice echoed, echoed, echoed.

The three boys bounced up and down on the leather seats as the song blasted. Chauncey shut the electronic window, separating him from the passenger compartment. He preferred a little Tommy Dorsey, who was now touring the country with Jackie Gleason and whom he saw at the Palladium in New York only the week before.

As they approached the house, the rain subsided, and Chauncey shut the windshield wipers off. The guard at the gate opened the massive wroth iron gates and the limo passed through. The columned mansion was visible through the barren branches of the many oak trees that lined the entrance. The entire mansion was pure white, which matched the white columned portico that covered a section of the circular driveway.

Chauncey pulled the limo under the portico, opened the rear door, and said, "You boys stay right there, I must talk to Master Sinclair alone."

He shut the door and walked about ten feet away from the car and said, "Master, I will drive your little friends home. I will tell them that your mum is sick and has requested that no visitors enter the house. They'll understand."

The little boy shook his head from side to side and said, "No, Chauncey, these are my friends, and I want to bring them into my home."

"Master, you don't understand, your father is home. He came home about an hour ago, and he is not in a very good mood," said Chauncey while pointing to the large mahogany front doors.

The boy began walking back toward the rear door of the limo, he stopped, grabbed Chauncey's hand, looked him sadly, and said, "Chauncey, you are my only friend, you feed me, you talk to me when I am sad, you tuck me in at night, but I want to have other friends. Kids my own age, kids that I can play with. Please, Chauce, please?" He rubbed his eye with his free hand while squeezing Chauncey's hand with the other. Chauncey now kneeled down and pulled the boy close to him. The boy hugged him and said, "Thanks, Chauncey, I love you."

The man was speechless. "You gather up your books, and your friends and I will go in first to clear the way."

Chauncey got up and briskly walked into the house just as the skies opened again with a furry. A combination of snow, rain, and sleet poured from the dark gray skies as the boy rushed to the limo. Claps of thunder could be heard as all hell broke loose in the skies. It was one of those New England days that down Easters talked about all summer. It was one of those clays that frightened even seasoned Yankees. It was Mother Nature at her worst.

The little boy rushed toward the front door with his friends in hot pursuit. He tried the door latch, but it was locked. He then began banging the brass door knocker over and over again, but still no one responded. Just then a rumble of thunder filled the air, and the boys began kicking at the door.

The lace curtain on the long slim window that buttressed the mahogany door was pulled back and Marlene, the servant's face, appeared. She was speaking but was not audible to the boy. He was trying to read her lips, couldn't make out even the simplest word.

The rumble of thunder finally subsided for a moment and he could hear Marlene say, "I cannot let you in. Do you hear me, I cannot let you in!"

"What? Why? What do you mean you cannot let me in?" shouted the boy.

"Your father gave me instructions not to let you in. He said that you had to find a way to get in on your own!" said the maid as she held the lace curtains aside as she pressed her lips against the glass.

"Please, Marlene, please let me in!" pleaded the boy, who now had tears in his eyes.

One of the two other boys turned and said, "Your family is nuts. I don't know why we came out here with you, you're all crazy. My dad told me about you people… I should have listened to him…he was right. Come on, Bobby, let's get out of here while we can."

The two boys picked up their books and ran down the circular drive way just as a thunderbolt flashed over their heads. One boy dropped his books on the wet drive way, quickly picked them up, and ran out of the wroth iron gate.

Crying the boy kicked the door as the dusk sky filled with bright flashes of light followed by loud claps of thunder. "Please, please let me in…I'm going to get struck by lightining… Please… Chauncey…you're my friend… Chaunce! God, please let me in!" cried the small boy as he pounded on hand and then the other on the huge mahogany door. The curtains were pulled back on the windows on both sides of the door, and peeking out with tears in their eyes were Chauncey and Marlene.

Shouting so he could be heard above the thunder, Chauncey cupped his hands over his mouth, "Your father said that you must find your own way in; we cannot help you."

The boy then ran to the side window, stood on his tip toes, and tried pushing up on the window pain. The windows were locked, and the run off from the roof gutter poured onto his head. He then went to four other windows, banged on the glass, and pushed up to no avail. The windows were all sealed shut, and the lace curtains were drawn. His little body shivered as the rain now saturated his outer and under clothes. Every time the cold breeze blew, his clothes felt like there were icy fingers squeezing his chest.

Another large thunder bolt lit up the entire side of the house. As the frightened little boy ran away from the house, he slipped and fell face first into a puddle of icy muddy water. His tears rolled down his cheeks and were brown as they fell from his chin. While getting up, he glanced up and saw his mother watching him from the second floor bedroom. She was signaling him with her hand. She was pointing toward the back of the house. He also noticed that she was crying. Very slowly she formed the words I LOVE YOU with her mouth. He then saw Father spin her around and pull down the shade. He could hear his father yelling at her, even with the window closed. Their silhouettes on the window shade were back lit by the overhead bedroom chandelier. He saw the silhouette of his father raise his hand and strike his mother's silhouette. Her silhouette suddenly disappeared from sight...

He ran to the back of the house as his mother had indicated. After running out of the rain and on to the back porch, he suddenly remembered that there was a small door that was installed for the dog. He got on his hands and knees and slowly squeezed his body through the tiny opening. His legs became jammed, but a frightened Chauncey, who was only feet away from him in the kitchen, stood there helplessly as the small boy cried out for help.

"Master Sinclair. I can't help you!" cried Chauncey as he wiped the tears from his eyes.

Standing at the other end of the large kitchen was his father with his arms crossed. Not saying a word but sending strong signals with his eyes, Chauncey stood like a paralyzed insect caught on fly paper.

Just as he squirmed the rest of his legs through, a loud gun shot rang out upstairs. The little boy, now free, ran past his father, up the stairs, and towards the bedroom.

By the time the others had followed him up the stairs, the little boy had already reached his mother and was cradling her blood splattered head in his arms.

CHAPTER 9

THE DARK ROOM WAS ILLUMINATED by a tiny glowing red dot that signaled that the radio was tuned in to a stereo station. The sweet sounds of Gerry Mulligan's trumpet were barely audible to him as he groped in the dark for a nearly empty water tumbler that contained red wine. His unsteady hand felt the glass, but in his inebriated state, he knocked it off of the small TV table and onto the rug. Holding on to the rocking chair with one hand, he bent over, picked up the glass, unscrewed the metal cap from the gallon of table wine by his side, and overfilled his glass. More wine dripped from the table and on to his stockinged foot. At four dollars a gallon, he wasn't concerned about spillage.

He gulped nearly half a glass before taking a breath, his eyes rolled back, and the bitter sweet wine rushed through his veins.

"Paris, 1985," he incoherently mumbled to himself as his mind raced back to a happier time.

"Fucking Paris, 1985," he yelled as he pushed his body back in the swaying rocker, its back slamming against the wall, which prevented him from tumbling backwards.

Images of the Eiffel Tower raced through his mind. Sitting at an outside cafe under a colorful Cezanne umbrella, with its bright red canvas frills gently flapping in the wind, he and his wife, with raised glasses, toasted their success.

The $200 bottle of Chateau Rothschild 1948 was soon consumed and replaced with a second. Their future looked as bright as the mid-afternoon sunlight that made the highlights in her blond hair seem like precious jewels. They then walked the Paris streets, kissing and embracing at every intersection, the warm spring dusk air caressed their faces and rustled their hair like gentle invisible fingers, slowly lifting and lowering each strand as though some unseen cherub had chosen them for all of his arrows of love.

In the hotel elevator, he pressed the emergency button, cupped her head in his hands, and kissed her with such passion that her body trembled. He then pressed his body against hers until they seemed as one. She was exploring his mouth with her tongue while wrapping her arms around his waist and pulling his body closer. As he then began to lift her skirt, the elevator phone began ringing without stop.

He then released the emergency button while still holding her. As the doors on the seventh floor opened, a small crowd of waiting individuals with angry faces suddenly began to smile as they looked at Jason's lipstick smeared face and Marnie's uplifted skirt. The two of them looked like Cheshire cats as she brushed her dress down and he wiped his face with his hand...only smearing it more. They then kissed as they walked toward their room.

Once in the room, their love making went on all night. There were no taboos that night. That evening he fell in love with the same woman for a second time. In the morning, as they embraced and sat staring at the Seine River, the yellow sun popping its head between the buildings looked like a child poking its head out of a birth canal. When the full yellow ball finally emerged from behind the skyline, they both felt as though they had just witnessed the inception of life. Aroused their tired and naked bodies joined again in a pagan celebration to another day of living.

It all seemed like a dream to him now as he poured himself another glass. He hadn't touched his wife in six months...he was relegated to the couch...with she locking herself into the bedroom each evening. His oldest daughter had moved to a friend's house and had not spoken to him in nearly three months. He knew that his wife would have done the same if she had a place to move to.

The dingy third floor tenement that they moved to was strewn with unpacked boxes that were arranged in such a way as to allow passage between rooms. The dark dirty rooms were a far cry from the hand painted ceilings in the portico of the Holden Mansion where they lived. As he sat there trying to lift his head that kept bobbing up and down, he also faced the realization that he couldn't even successfully take his own life.

Three failed attempts had humiliated his family and ostracized his confirmation aged daughter from the Catholic Church. After her catechism priest condemned her dad in front of thirteen other children for attempting to take his own life, she verbosely came to his defense. She then wrote a very emotional letter to the Monsignor defending her dad and condemning the priest. The Monsignor was so incest that he sent word through the parish priest that she and her family were no longer welcomed in that parish. The priest also called the house and told Marnie that if any member of the family approached the altar during mass while he was serving the Eucharist that he would refuse it to them.

This devastated Marnie, who apparently decided at that time that Jason no longer deserved her support or help. She would no longer come to his rescue when she discovered his unconscious body next to empty pill and wine bottles.

She told him, "Jay, you want to die, then why don't you do it right and get yourself a gun. Just don't do it in the apartment...you've put the kids and me through enough trauma."

For a short period of time, she even began leaving full bottles of over the counter sleeping pills in his underwear draw and near his electric shaver. The not so subtle message was one that Jason anguished over deeply. He knew that she would be better off without him. She was still young enough to find someone who could fill her financial, emotional, and physical needs. He felt that that thought had also crossed her mind.

Before marrying Jason, she used to date Chuck, an automobile mechanic. Jason used to call him a grease monkey and a loser. The man went on to buy his own Japanese auto dealership and is considered one of the wealthiest men in the community. Maybe Chucky would come out of the wood work if Jason decided to eat some lead. For some reason, Jason just could not bring himself to do it. Maybe it was the primal instinct of self-preservation, maybe it was in defiance to Marnie, maybe it was because of his widowed father, or just maybe it was the simple lack of courage. For whatever reason, he chose a coward's form of self-destruction.

He poisoned his body every day with cheap wine and over the counter tranquilizers. His seventy-nine-year-old father, who was never sparing in his unrequested dissemination of advice, told him "Jay, with the financial mess that you are in, you have one problem... By drinking you now have two problems...if your wife should leave you because of your drinking...you will then have three problems...so please stop your drinking "

He would tell his father, "Pop, this is not your problem or decision, it's mine."

His father would look at him with those sad puppy dog eyes and say, "Since your mother died, you are all I have; if you die, I'll die. Things will get better. You've got a job at that place...Bigel-."

Jason would look at him with his glassy eyes and ask him, "Pop, have you ever been to hell? I go and work there every night...every fucking night."

In his stupor, his hatred turned to Bigelows. They had denigrated him and reduced him to a sub-human life form that existed on fear, hate, and pity. His once creative mind that blossomed ideas like budding flowers in spring was now saturated in alcohol and functioned at a primordial level...festering like a puss infected wound.

He reached for his glass and gulped its contents. He then lifted the gallon to pour another drink but realized that he had consumed the entire gallon.

"I've got to take a piss," he whispered to himself as he attempted unsuccessfully to get out of the rocking chair. He fell back, passed out, and uncontrollably urinated in his pants. The urine formed a dark patch on his khaki pants and dripped down the wooden dowels of the rocker and into the rug where it mingled with the spilt wine.

The overhead light went on, and there stood his wife holding her hand over her nose, more in disgust than in disbelief.

His body jarred slightly as he regained partial conscientious only to hear her quivering voice say, "You are pathetic, you are really pathetic!" before lapsing back into his alcohol induced deep sleep.

At four in the morning, he was jolted awake by the ringing phone. He reached down, fumbled with the receiver, and a mumbled voice said, "Yeah...hello...ah."

"Say, man, where the fuck were you last night, man...?"

"Lenny, is that you?" mumbled Jason.

Who the fuck do you think it is...your fairy godmother?"

"I... I wasn't feeling very well... I was sick... I..."

"Fuck you, Jason...you got fucked up again, didn't you...you got all fucked up!" yelled Lenny while switching the phone to his other ear.

"I can't begin to thank you, Lenny...you are my frien...."

"Fuck you, Jason...I'm sick and fucking tired of covering your ass...this is the last time...you hear me, you mother fucker...the last fucking time."

"Lenny, you're a real friend...are you on your break?" asked Jason.

"You listen to me...last night Rasha got hurt real bad... I mean bad...they took him outta here about 3 A.M...the fucking medics had to give him CPR... they told us that he had an asthma attack.. man...fucking Rasha don't have no fucking asthma...man, I've known him for five years...he never told me about no fucking asthma."

"Lenny, I'm sorry. Is there anything that I can...."

"He went into the shit house and it happened there... Jack told me that two guards went in there. The bastards claimed that they found him on the floor...passed out...but those lying cocksuckers did it to him... Rasha was spying for you and they caught him," said Lenny with a nervous quiver in his voice.

"Lenny, are you saying that it was my fault?" asked Jason while holding his throbbing head.

"Listen, man...we gotta do some talkin'... I mean I'm probably next... I mean those pricks are probably watchin' me right now and listenin' to me...we gotta talk..." said Lenny nervously while cupping the phone in an attempt at shielding his words.

"When?" asked Jason.

"Today...you hear me...fucking today!" yelled Lenny while slamming the receiver, which caused a sharp pain to shoot across Jason's head.

Lenny had covered for Jason on a number of occasions by calling the security desk from a pay phone, telling them that he was Jason, and reporting that he wouldn't be in due to sickness. The last call that he made covering for Jason, Lenny said that his mother-in-law had passed away without even realizing that Jason's mother-in-law had died three years ago.

After having two cups of black coffee and three aspirins, he washed his unshaven face and tried to leave the house before Marnie rose. There was nothing to talk about, and apologies were as ineffectual as excuses.

But before he could slide out of the back door, she suddenly appeared and said, "Jay, we've got to talk. We just can't go on like this...it's not fair...not to you...and not to me."

"Yea, we'll talk... Marn...we'll talk latter. Right now there is something very wrong at Bigelows, and I've got to get to the bottom of it. Something very wrong."

"Jay, there is something very wrong here... Can't you see it, it has nothing to do with Bigelows."

"You're wrong, Marnie, it has everything to do with Bigelows. People are dying there, and they are trying to kill me...something evil is trying to do me in... Marnie, it's a force...that's ruined my life."

With a genuinely sympathetic smile on her face, she said, "Jay, you need some professional help. You are losing it and blaming it on Bige..."

Jay grabbed and squeezed both of her arms and said, "God damned it, Marnie, you just don't get it, do you? You just don't get it."

"You're hurting me, Jay, now let go...now," said Marnie while trying to avoid eye contact with Jay. "You didn't go in last night again, now did you?" asked Marnie while trying to change to subject.

He loosened his grip and raised her head with his hand until their eyes met, "I know that I've put you and the kids through a meat grinder, and I wouldn't blame you for leaving if that is what you thought was right thing to do, but I think that my life is in danger...and I think that it has something to do with that hell hole that I work in."

"Jay, I think that you've gone crazy. I think that the pills and booze have finally corroded whatever is left of your brain."

"Marnie, please believe me, something is very wrong there, and I'm going to get to the bottom of it," pleaded Jason.

"If what you are saying is true, then what proof do you have...those accidents... I mean maybe those people just have lousy coordination. Maybe they try to work without getting enough sleep and end up hurting themselves. Maybe they're all drunks like you," said Marnie. "Just what are you getting at, Jay? Can you hear yourself? I mean you drink yourself into a coma, skip work, and come up with some harebrained idea that someone is trying to kill you in an effort at trying to evoke some sympathy out of me. Maybe someone is trying to kill you, and maybe it's one of our many creditors who have finally figured out that you are not good for any of the money that you owe them and would rather do you in than let you go around telling everyone that you screwed them. Jay, I don't have any of the answers, and neither do you," said Marnie while walking toward the coffee pot on the stove.

"Marnie, please help me. I love you," said Jay while walking after her.

"Please, Jay, don't insult my intelligence. The only reason that I'm staying in this stinking house with you is that I have nowhere to go and you know it! So don't give me that shit about love. Don't turn my stomach the first thing in the morning. We're beyond that now," said Marnie while pouring herself a cup of coffee. "You know, Jay, there are nights that I sit up in bed, the smell of beer coming from your opened snoring mouth, your face unshaven, and your clothes reeking from sweat and vomit. You know I sit there and think of ways of killing you myself. Maybe a pillow over your head, maybe throwing your electric shaver into the shower when you finally decide to take one, maybe a sudden blow to the head....and blame it on a drunken fall."

"You're kidding, right?" asked Jason while rubbing the bridge of his nose with his right hand as he so often does when he gets nervous.

"Sure, I'm kidding, you've been such a great guy lately, why would thoughts like that ever cross my mind. On the other hand, maybe deep inside that I'm hoping what you told me about Bigelows is true."

Jason put on his coat and left the apartment without saying another word to Marnie. Her words still ringing in his ears as he leaped down the stairs...two at a time. His focus was now clear. He sat behind the wheel of his car, thinking about where he could go to get information. What Marnie didn't understand was that it wasn't only his life but also Lenny's that was in danger. Information...he needed information.

Where in the hell am I going to get some information, he thought as he put the key in the ignition, started the car, and drove off.

He decided to begin at the Bridgewater public library. Why not. If they didn't have what he was looking for, then someone there could probably point him in the right direction.

As he drove, his mind drifted to Bigelows again.

After TJ's death, Jason went into a deep depression. An evil force was treating humans like Pavlovian creatures in some kind of sick experiment. After TJ's death, he was sure that the source of all of this evil was Bigelows. It lived in that factory...its eyes and tentacles reached out into every corner and intruded into everyone's privacy, spying, probing, manipulating the poor souls that performed like trained circus dogs in center stage. He carried a small arsenal of lucky charms and wore a talisman to ward off the negative spirit that he felt surrounded him. He desperately clung to his perception of reality. That perception was now tainted with superstition and an overall belief that universal forces were working in harmony against him.

The cameras peeled away the fragile layers of dignity and exposed scared and obedient servants whose acquiescence further increased the degree of manipulation. An increasing number of workers were injured as they attempted to maneuver through places with protruding pipes and low hanging overhead partitions. Eyes were gouged out, lacerations were common and frequent, and the cement floor was stained with dried blood like that of a battle field.

Security cameras bobbed back and forth as EMTs removed injured workers on stretchers. Every accident was explained away as employee carelessness. OSHA inspectors were given detailed explanations of major accidents, in which they indicated that warning and danger signs were ignored by workers. When word was received of an impending inspection, the mazes were eliminated and all of the proper warning signs were posted.

At one location, numerous memento and flowers were placed over a blood-stained section of cement floor to mark the spot as does the wreath at the tomb of the unknown soldier. Even though the floor had been scrubbed clean, the tell-tale blood stain still appeared like an apparition giving a warning. Its brown presence kept reappearing. The half dozen daffodils that were discretely placed on the stained spot one evening were quickly gathered up by security guards and placed into plastic bags. They looked like cops gathering evidence at a crime scene.

For some reason, injured employees did not sue the company. A rumor circulated about an injured employee who began a letter writing campaign about the mazes, which led to his debilitating accident. He was supposedly visited at his home by three burly men in expensive suits while his wife was shopping.

Ten minutes alone with the men and the employee refused to discuss his accident or Bigelows to anyone. He never did return to work and quietly moved to an undisclosed location…supposedly for his health.

Jason felt like a Skinnerian rat. He had to constantly remind himself that he is a Harvard graduate with an IQ of 135. With his self-respect and self-esteem moving closer to a black hole, he had to utilize all of his remaining strength to keep his destiny from falling into someone else's hands…someone who indiscriminately inflicts pain while remaining anonymous. Someone evil.

"Go on, eat the apple…go on…and I'll make your life a living hell… Go on, Adam, just one bite. What's one bite," kept on going through his mind while he was driving.

The one thing that he valued more than anything was beginning to elude him. His intelligence was all that he had left. It was the only thing that separated him from all others. The delusionary states that his fragile mind experienced lately made him wonder about the status of his mental well-being. He was cursed…a diabolical creature had intervened into his idyllic life and imposed pennants that befit no crime that he had ever committed. Even his few moral transgressions would never have justified the crucifixion he had endured.

The apple…go on, just one small bite, he thought again as he sped towards the library.

He would leave Bigelows at six thirty in the morning with a feeling as though he had defied the odds for another eight hours. With his material possessions gone, his wife wishing that he were dead, his reputation shot to hell, and his company bankrupt, he was now being forced to sell his soul to the devil for $6.00 an hour.

He always had a convoluted way of looking at money. He regarded money as pieces of his life. Each possession represented hours that he had given up in order to earn cash. The more expensive the item, the more hours given up. Hours that he could never again recover. Hours that were gone forever. Now that most of his material possessions were gone, so were chunks of his life that he expended in order to purchase these items. With most of everything gone, so was most of his life. So his equation went.

Most of his personal possessions had been sold off at yard sales. People bickering about paying fifty cents for a silk tie that had cost him forty-five dollars. He would often get into a verbal sparing contest with his yard sale customers.

"You cheap bastard," he said to a balding yard sale customer who told him that his first edition of Emanuel Velikovsky's "World in Collision" was not worth five dollars when he had paid $150 for it at a booksmith. "You drive in here with a $45,000 Lexus and try to screw me out a five bucks. Get the hell out of here, you cheap prick."

His dream home had been sold by the bank for pennies on the dollar at a public auction. His children watched the auctioneer from their second story bedroom window, tears in their eyes as a complete stranger made the final bid. The sheriff served them with an eviction notice that afternoon. It was shortly thereafter when his oldest daughter told him that she endured enough embarrassment…she was moving to her friend's home. He knew that she was an innocent victim in all of this. The day that she moved, he felt as though a large piece of him died...and it did.

After she moved out, he thought of killing himself. As he drove to work that night, he had the impulse to steer his van into oncoming traffic and end it all.

Come on, Adam...no one will know...taste the fruit... one small bite won't change anything, he thought as he drove towards Bridgewater.

He now focused on Bigelows as the antithesis of all of his values. He knew that a diabolical force treated those poor bastards like play soldiers on an Astroturf battlefield. Many of these employees were ex-cons whose probation officers would more than likely put them back into the can if they quit. Many of the others were immigrants from either Portugal or China who spoke very little English and who regarded $6.00 an hour like manna from heaven.

Continuity of their visas were contingent upon being gainfully employed. Therefore they tolerated the intolerable with a tenacious and pioneer spirit... not knowing that these conditions were not prevalent at any other company in the United States. They all functioned like puppets on a string, nodding and smiling, following the yellow taped mazes through dangerous twists and turns, completely oblivious to the spying cameras and heavy-handed security guards.

These poor souls, ignorant in their own culture, were fodder for this cunning new world force. Tender specimens to be microscopically examined by cameras as they performed ritualistic acts of work as bees serving the queen.

One evening the maze led to the second story of the warehouse. The yellow taped highway continued into a large clump of clothes suspended on racks beyond, which was a one-story drop. An oriental man anxious to get to his work station before the starting bell sounded pushed the clothes aside and blindly proceeded. He plunged off of the landing and lay unconscious on the pavement below, his head bleeding profusely.

A contingent of other Asians rushed to his side. Not to assist him in his injuries but to revive him before a supervisor arrived on the scene and fired him. A supervisor did arrive and stood stoically beside the injured man with his arms folded with indifference. After regaining consciousness, an interpreter translated the man's first words. They were addressed to his supervisor....

"I sorry for this...it not happen again... I fine...please return to work...no fire...please no fire."

The man got up with the assistance of his friends and hobbled to his work site...his head still covered with blood.

Jason knew that he had to do something. Instead of drinking and sleeping days, he told himself that he must now spend his time gathering information about Bigelows. Because it was a family corporation, he realized that getting corporate information would be difficult, if not impossible. He would then pursue whatever public information that the Bridgewater public library had to offer and begin to strategize his next move from there.

As he entered the center of town, the library was conspicuous by its overbearance. Its presence dominated what little architecture existed in the town square. The large building resembled a miniature Parthenon sitting on a small hill overlooking the town. Its large Roman columns supported large slabs of cut granite into which were carved the words, "The People's University." In a blue-collar community such as this, it was the people's university. A bronze statue of a caped man holding a walking stick stood near the entrance of the library. The statute had turned green with age and was covered with pigeon droppings. It seemed to be staring at some fixed object located somewhere across the town square.

Jason entered the library and went to the main desk where a grayed haired woman in her sixties gawked at him above her half glasses that rested at the end of her long nose.

"Can I do something for you, young man?" asked the lady as she casually pushed her hair back with one hand while removing her glasses with the other.

"Well, yes, you can. Do you have a microfilm library of local newspaper articles?" asked Jason while looking at her bright blue eyes, which seemed to emanate a wildness that existed beyond the smoldering embers.

The woman leaned toward Jason while supporting her head with her hand, a look on her face that said take me, take me. "The reference room is on the second floor...is there anything else I can do for you?" she said now with a coy smile on her face.

Jason, not wanting to encourage her, turned away from, began walking, and said, "Thank you, ma'am."

He was greeted by a young black woman, with her hair cut shorter than his, with what appeared to be a pop rivet in her nose.

"Can I be of any help?" she asked without looking up from the form that she was filling out on her desk.

"Yes, I would like some information about a family known as Bigelow... I understand that you have micro film records of the local newspaper... Am I right?" asked Jason.

"What type of information are you interested in?" she asked while putting down her Cross pen and looking up at him with her large brown eyes.

"I am interested in any information that you may have regarding the Bigelow family," he said abruptly.

"Well, there is only one Bigelow clan in Bridgewater...you must be talking about the seed people...why, it is widely known that they built and own most of this town..." the woman said, now rising and looking Jason straight in the eye.

"No kidding," he said.

"Everyone knows that...say you're not from these parts, are you?" asked the librarian.

"No, I'm not," said Jason.

"Why, the Bigelow family even donated the money to build this library in 1935...right in the middle of the Depression....the Bigelows are local celebrities around here," said the librarian in a sarcastic manner while walking over to the window and signaling Jason to follow.

Pointing out of the window, the librarian said, "You see that statute down there that looks like Count Dracula?...Well, that's Christian Bigelow...this library was named after him and was built with Bigelow money in memory of him," said the librarian, now with a sort of curious look on her face. She leaned forward and whispered to Jason, "He died of syphilis at the age of nineteen, as a matter of fact, did you notice the bell tower on the library roof?"

"No, I didn't," said Jason.

"Well, one of the stipulations of the bequest was that the bell would have to be rung every day at exactly 11:26 in the morning. That was the exact time that Christian died. The bell hasn't been rung for nearly thirty years...ever since our building inspector noticed cracks in the tower supports. The surviving Bigelows were agreeable to silencing the bell since they regarded its daily ringing as a cruel joke," said the librarian while moving back to her desk.

"That's all very interesting but..." said Jason as he was interrupted midsentence.

"You know the local town folks liked the Bigelows for one reason and one reason only...money," said the librarian in a tone that was barely audible. She signaled him to come closer as she kept staring both at the ceiling and at the entrance door to see if anyone was within hearing distance. "They owned this town then and they own this town now."

"Are you talking about that factory?" whispered Jason.

"I'm talking about everything... They still run this town and all of its people... Have you ever been in that factory?" whispered the librarian.

"As a matter of fact, I work in that factory...that's the reason why I am here. I want to find out who runs that place. Can you give me any information about the Bigelows who operates that place?" asked Jason while rubbing the bridge of his nose.

The woman disappeared into the stacks and returned about five minutes later with three micro films.

"December 23rd, 1955, July 16th, 1962, and January 10th, 1993, I think you'll find some interesting information in these tapes," said the woman with a knowing smirk on her face as she handed the plastic containers to Jason.

Jason went to the viewing machine and fed the tape in the receptacle. He stopped the image on the screen to see where he was on the film and then quickly advanced it until the front page of the 21st appeared. He then slowly advanced it until the December 23rd front page headline of the Gazette appeared.

"Rose Bigelow – Dead"

Jason quickly adjusted the focusing lever on the machine and began reading the article, "According to those present, Mrs. Rose Bigelow has died as a result of a gun accident. Her body was found by Sinclair Bigelow, her eleven-year-old son. According to her husband, she was apparently in the process of relocating the fire arm that was kept in the master bedroom to a safer location when the accident occurred. In a call to the District Attorney office, he indicated that his office will conduct an investigation, but there is no reason to doubt the recollections given by Mr. Bigelow and the house staff. Mr. Bigelow is the owner and operator of the Bigelow seed company of Bridgewater."

Jason pushed the copy button on the viewer and turned to subsequent days to see if there were any follow up articles. There were none. It was as though the story was squashed.

He then put the July 16th, 1962 tape into the machine and proceeded to that front page. The headline read, "Winslow Bigelow Disappears." The article stated Winslow Bigelow, local businessman, mysteriously disappeared while on his way to his company... The Bigelow Seed Factory. The FBI and local officials are working together on this case, and any information to the press will be released through the Boston office of the Federal Bureau of Investigation."

Jason pressed the copy button and then checked the newspapers for the 17th and 18th and found follow-up stories but with no resolution of the disappearance. The follow-up stories stated that Sinclair Bigelow would now assume full control of the Bigelow company and holdings. He quickly rewound the tape and put in the tape of January 1993. He turned to January 10th and found no startling headlines. He then slowly turned to pages one, two, three, four, and finally to the business section on page five. There without a picture was a story about Sinclair Bigelow. "S. Bigelow Appointed to Board."

As Jason read on, his heart began beating faster, and beads of perspiration formed on his forehead. His eyes twitched nervously as he read, "Sinclair Bigelow received the unanimous vote of the Board of Directors of the Flaggstaff Company to serve on its Board. One of Mr. Bigelow's first duties will be to serve as Chairman of the Contracts Review Committee."

His trembling hand pressed the copy button as he tried to compose himself.

Under his voice but loud enough for the librarian to hear, he said, "It was that son of a bitch who cancelled my contract... I know it...and now he's trying to kill me!"

The female librarian rushed over and placed her hand on his shoulder and whispered, "Please, you must keep it down. If you want me to help you, you must act as though everything is OK."

"I'm sorry, what is your name?" asked Jason.

"Ms. Rogers…now listen to me carefully…"

"No, you listen to me, Ms. Rogers. Is there a pay phone in here?" asked Jason.

"Yes, on the first floor near the front entrance," said Ms. Rogers, now standing up and hoping that Jason left and didn't return.

He raced to the phone, put in all the change requested by the operator and heard, "Hello, Flaggstaff Company, do you know your extension…if so press it now."

Jason pushed 604 and waited. "Hello, Mr. Saunders' office, whom shall I say is calling?"

"Jason Burns," said Jason impatiently.

"Well, how in the hell are you, Jay?"

"Listen, cut the shit, Tom, I need to know who delivered that cancelled contract to my office!" demanded Jason.

"Jay, are you still brooding about that incident?" asked Tom.

"Tom, I'm on a pay phone and I don't have time to bullshit with you, now who in the hell delivered that contract!" yelled Tom while searching in his pants pockets for more change in anticipation of a request from the operator.

"I believe that that was Sheila Cochran, yes…I'm certain it was her," said Tom as the pitch of his voice dropped to a much calmer level.

"Tom, please connect me to her extension… It is very important that I speak with her," pleaded Jason while depositing an extra twenty-five cents into the slot after the operator's request.

Tom's voice was abruptly cut off by the ringing of the extension.

"Hello, Sheila Cochrane speaking."

"Ms. Cochrane, this is Jason Burns speaking, do you remember me?" asked Jason in a calm and nonobtrusive voice.

"No, I'm sorry that I don't… Who are you, Mr. Burns, and what can I do for you?" asked Ms. Cochran.

"Think back to the spring of 1993...delivering a contract cancellation letter to a company called the Creative Factory in Fall River."

"Ah, no, I'm sorry, Mr. Burns...I don't recall..."

"The think tank room...the glass enclosed room."

"Oh, yes, now I remember. You guys looked like fish in a tank. Your secretary wouldn't let me in for some reason. Yes, I remember...there was an oriental man talking to you. Is that what you wanted to know, Mr. Burns?" asked Ms. Cochron.

"No, what I would like to know is who instructed you to create that letter...who made that decision?" asked Jason without trying to appear overly anxious with her answer. There was silence on the other end of the line. "Was it Mr. Bigelow?" asked Jason with a hint of impatience in his voice. "I know that it was Mr. Bigelow," said Jason in a very confident tone.

"If you know that it was Mr. Bigelow, then why are you asking me?" said Ms. Cochron in a tone that indicated to Jason that she might hang up.

"Then it was Mr. Bigelow," insisted Jason. "It was Mr. Bigelow, now wasn't it...it was, wasn't it...it was...it was," repeated Jason with an escalating tone of impatience in his voice.

"All right it was," shouted Ms. Cochron, who then slammed the phone as if to negate her confession.

Jason could feel his blood pressure rising as he slowly placed the receiver back on to the chromium receiver. He composed himself and then returned to the reference room.

A look of anxiety flashed across Ms. Rogers' face when Jason entered the room. His hand was trembling, and he had a crazed look in his eyes that wasn't there before.

"Ms. Rogers," he said in a surprisingly calm voice, "I've got to know more about Sinclair Bigelow."

"Like what?" asked Ms. Rogers.

Jason began rubbing the bridge of his nose and said, "I want to know where he lives, what he eats for breakfast, what he drives, I want to know everything that you apparently seem to know about him and his family."

Ms. Rogers signaled him to join her at a round table at the far end of the reference room. He folded his photo copies and placed them into his inner pocket when a matronly-looking woman rushed into the room and stood next to them and very abruptly asked, "Is there something that I can help you with, young man?"

"Ah, well..." said Jason.

"Miss Rogers, why don't you report to the first floor... I will take care of this matter," said the woman who now had folded her arms and was looking at Jason as though he had violated an enemy fortress.

The black librarian looked rankled as she grabbed her pocket-book, her coat, and left abruptly without looking at either Jason or the woman.

"My name is Miss Sylvia. What is yours?"

"My name is Rodney Smith," said Jason in a sarcastic tone.

"Don't play games with me, Mr. Burns," said Ms. Sylvia.

"If you know who I am, then why in the hell did you ask me my name?" yelled Jason.

"Don't play games with me, Mr. Burns...what is it that you want?" demanded Mrs. Sylvia.

"Answer me two questions," said Jason.

"What are they, Mr. Burns?" asked Miss Sylvia as she slowly walked over the card file while nervously fidgeting with her lace collar.

"Number one, who operates the Bigelow plant on a day to day basis, and number two, why are those surveillance cameras pointed at us," asked Jason while staring at three ceiling mounted cameras that were now all pointed in their direction.

"Mr. Smith, I think that it is time for you to leave."

"Miss Sylvia, I need some answers, and I am not going to leave until I get them!" exclaimed Jason while waving his index finger at her.

Miss Sylvia reached for the phone and shouted, "I am calling security and having you removed!"

Jason reached for her hand and held it on the telephone receiver. "You are not calling anyone until I get some god-damned answers! Now who is in charge of the fucking plant!"

Just then two of what appeared to be men in gray suits entered the room and walked abruptly toward Jason. As they came closer, he noticed the protrusions in their shirts and realized that they were women. He tried to resist as they grabbed him under the arm pits and hauled him off...his feet kicking but not touching the floor He was taken into a service elevator where he was held by one hermaphrodite and beaten by the other. One of them threw the emergency switch as the elevator jolted to an abrupt stop.

He tried to take a swing, but his fist was grabbed and crushed. The pain was excruciating. Before he could jar his head, a sudden punch to his nose left him semi-conscious. He could feel the warm blood dripping down his face as he felt the elevator begin to move downward.

He was carried to the back alley and thrown against a dumpster. Laying there trying to gain his composure, he could smell the rotting garbage and could hear the rats scurrying. He made it to his feet and hobbled to his car.

He noticed a piece of paper under the windshield wiper. While holding a handkerchief up to his nose to catch the blood, he read the note.

"879-8442 - tonight!"

CHAPTER 10

HIS HEAD FELT AS THOUGH A THOUSAND-POUND WEIGHT had been dropped on it from the top floor of the Empire State building. The booze and the beating he had taken that day had numbed his senses to the point where his incoherence bordered on schizophrenia. His pillow was covered with blood, which was now crusted on his face, his body reeked of cheap bourbon and perspiration, and his head felt like a pin ball machine, hitting random points in his mind that conjured up disturbing images.

A voice deep in his psyche kept telling him to focus, but his 33 1/3 thoughts were now racing at 78 rpms. He moved his head back and forth gyroscopically in an attempt at focusing his thoughts. He raised his body into a sitting position, reached into his pocket, and groped for a tissue to remove some of the crusted blood from his nose. While removing the tissue, a small piece of crumbled paper fell to the floor. He uncrumpled it, stared at it, and closed his eyes.

He thought that he would suddenly awaken, roll to his side, and see his beautiful wife cocooned in her satin sheets.. gently awake her and tell her about the terrible nightmare that he just had. She would then kiss him gently on his forehead, entwine him in her clutches, and they would make passionate love until the morning alarm went off.

He suddenly realized that this nightmare was real. He opened his eyes and slowly focused them on the paper that was wedged between his first and second figures. It just sat there like a foreign object. His mind now conjured up images of the library, the black librarian, the two creatures that beat him senseless, and the message that he found on the windshield...

"It had to be that Ms. Rogers from the reference room," he thought as he dialed the number.

Her phone rang three times before her recorded voice spoke mechanically on the answering machine and said, "I am sorry that we can't come to the phone right now. At the sound of the beep, leave your name and number and we'll get back to you."

"My name is Jason Burns, and I got the message that you left on my car wind...."

The message was cut off abruptly and a faint female voice said, "My name is Marylin Rogers from the..."

"From the library," Jason interrupted. "What the hell is going on....and who were those two female sumo wrestler who rearranged my nose?" asked Jason indignantly.

"Jason, I can't talk on the phone...we are both in danger, along with everyone in that plant. Before you go to work tonight, I must talk to you," said Ms. Rogers at a whisper.

"I'm not going in tonight. That place can go screw itself, excuse my French. I'm done, Ms. Roger. I'm throwing in the god damned towel; my life is a horror show, and it's getting worse every day. I decided to..."

"I don't give a damn what you decided to do, you self-centered asshole. Didn't you hear me when I said that our lives are in danger! Our lives, not just yours! Our little tete ta tete today has put me and my family in grave danger, and you are not going to leave me hanging out there. Do you understand?"

"No, I don't understand. I think that you are a little paranoid and..."

"You know something, Burns? You're walking around with your head up your butt. You really don't care, do you? You don't care about me...you don't care about those people in that plant...you don't care about anything except your own personal agenda! How many of your Bigelow friends are missing or dead? One, two, three, a half a dozen, a dozen, two dozen…? Did it ever occur to you that maybe you're next? Maybe your family? I assume that you have a family, or maybe I'm taking a giant leap of faith there." There was silence on the phone. "Are you still there?" asked Ms. Rogers.

"You made your point, Rogers, now where do you want to meet and when?" blurted Jason while switching the phone to the other ear.

"I'll meet you at my sister's house in Brockton. She and her family are attending her mother-in-law's funeral in Georgia, and I have the key. Also, no one from the library knows where she lives. It's at 235 Westwood Street, second floor. Come up the back stairs. The front is usually locked. Be there at 8:30 tonight before you go into work," said Ms. Rogers while jotting down her own instructions into a small notebook.

"Rogers, I'm going in tonight and quitting," said Jason.

"The hell you're are. You can't quit, you must go back there…and you must go back as though nothing happened. You're going to work with me to get to the bottom of this and find out what the hell is going on. You're in too deep, Burns…after the library incident, they've got your number."

"You don't seem to understand. That bastard ruined my life, and I'm not going to spend another day in…"

"Ruined your life? My mother was a servant in the Bigelow house for ten years until one day she came home and hanged herself from the shower nozzle in the tub. I was thirteen when I found her. I spent the next five years bouncing from one foster home to another and from one psychologist to another…so don't give me that crap about ruining your life!" said Ms. Rogers as her voiced quivered.

"Gee, I'm sorry, Ms. Rogers, I had no…"

"Save your sympathy, Burns. I've already said too much over the phone. I'll tell you what I know tonight. Someone's at the door, I've got to go."

"Another thing," Jason said almost apologetic. "Who in the hell beat me up today? Animal, vegetable, or mineral?" He could hear banging in the back ground.

She ignored his question and said impatiently, "Now I've got to answer the door before they break the door down. I'll see you tonight at 8:30. If you decide not to show up, don't bother trying to contact me again. Do you understand?" asked Ms. Rogers while hanging up the receiver before he could respond.

Jason showered, shaved, and put on a casual set of work clothes. It was 8:00 P.M., and Brockton was only a half hour away. He hated Brockton and tried to avoid it whenever he could. It had a reputation of street violence and drive by shootings that gave it the dubious distinction of being the crime capital of New England. But nothing there could even compare to the violence that he had experienced in the last ninety days.

Traffic was light on route twenty-four at this time of night, and her directions were good. He reached Westwood Street by 8:20 and parked his car in the back of one that had a bumper sticker that read "Free Porto Rico." He glanced up to the second floor and saw that the apartment was in darkness. Perhaps she had forgotten, perhaps she dozed off.

At 8:30 he walked toward the front stairs. He glanced up and thought that these three-story tenement houses were typical for this area. When the mills were turning out garments and shoes around the clock, mill workers rented living quarters in these houses, so they could walk to work. In those days, many of them were owned by the mills who deducted rent from the laborers weekly pay. He remembered his dad telling him about the sweat shop that he worked in where he made $11.50 a week.

He started walking up the front stairs when he remembered what she told him. He turned around and walked into the back yard. There was no moon out, and he groped around in pitch darkness to find the down stairs door knob leading to a dark hall.

He knew that her tenement was on the second floor but could see no light escaping from the crevices that separated the old door from the threshold.

He knocked, but no one answered. He knocked again, this time harder than the first. He then turned the door knob, and the door swung open.

As he entered he asked, "Ms. Rogers, are you here? Ms. Rogers? It's Jason."

He blindly reached around for the light switch, which he assumed would be right next to the back door. He felt it with his hand and flipped the switch up.

As he glanced around to the illuminated kitchen table, his heart began beating rapidly, and his eyes looked on in disbelief. There on a plate in the middle of the table was the severed head of Ms. Rogers, her eyes were still open, and her mouth was frozen in mid-sentence...as though she had attempted to scream some words of warning while she was brutally murdered.

He began trembling as he approached the grotesque site. His eyes then focused on to a hunting knife that jutted out of the top of her head. Blood overflowed the platter onto the table and was slowly dripping into a puddle on the flowered linoleum floor. The blade of the knife was stuck through a piece of paper, which read, "Jason...you must find your way alone."

His body trembled as he sprung backwards in an attempt at putting some distance between him and this horrible sight. When he did, he slipped on a pool of blood that dripped from the table. The thick red substance covered the soles of his sneakers, creating a slimy film. As both of his feet slid from under him, his hand swung out, hitting the head and sending it flying from the plate. It hit the floor with a thump and rolled like a soccer ball. While it rolled, he could hear the knife tapping the floor...thump...thump... thump...before it came to rest against the opposite wall. Her eyes staring at him, the severed nerves and arteries jutting out of her jaggedly cut neck.

He got up and ran down the stairs. His hands were covered in blood. He wiped them on his coat before he approached his car. Two young Porto Ricans were sitting on his hood, smoking and talking. They nonchalantly glanced at him as he approached and then continued their conversation.

He ignored them, got in the car, revved the engine as a warning, which they didn't heed, and sped off. He could hear them swearing at him, "You fucking idiot," after they pushed themselves off at the first intersection. Both were jumping up and down and waving their fingers in the air as he pushed the accelerator to the floor and created a screeching sound that could be heard for blocks.

While he sped up the high way, he thought of the first time that he visited his mother's grave after she had been buried. The funeral was in the morning, but he drove back to the cemetery in the middle of night. The main gates were locked, so he left his car, hopped over the stone wall, and walked nearly a quarter of a mile to her grave. The dirt was fresh over the four by ten rectangle that had been neatly cut out of the manicured grass. He got on his hands and knees and began digging. She was only a small fragile lady of ninety-three pounds, and he wanted to remove all of the dirt from the top of her. He also wanted to dig her up and hold her one last time. She had a secret name for him...no one but she called him that...and she never used it in front of anyone else. He just wanted to hold her and have her call him Butch, just one last time... Butch... I love you, Butch... He could feel the cold, moist dirt between his fingers as he frantically pushed the soil aside. He remembered how his tears fell freely onto the dirt and how he threw himself prostrate on to the moist fresh soil, his body shaking as he cried. He felt the same pain now.

Images of Roger's contorted face filled his mind as he sped towards Bigelows. Instead of her face, he could see his mother's face sitting on the table with her eyes opened and her lips moving silently forming the word Butch... Butch... Butch.

He was pushing his car as fast as it could go. He knew that he must get to the plant and warn them that they are all in danger. Yes, it was all up to him.

He could hear his mother's voice whispering... Jason, save them... Butch, save them... Butch....save them.

CHAPTER 11

BEADS OF SWEAT ROLLED OFF OF HIS FOREHEAD and into his eyes, stinging them with its salty nectar. The speedometer read ninety-seven miles per hour, but his mind raced even faster. It was not him steering that car, it was someone else, someone who was impregnable to pain, someone who had a mission with a wind mill, someone whom even he didn't recognize as himself. He glanced into the rearview mirror, but it wasn't adjusted, but it didn't matter because his glance, like his driving, was a programmed mechanical response that was being performed by a part of his brain that had nothing to do with his conscious level.

He swerved his car into a convenience store parking lot after getting off of the highway, nearly hit one of the gas pumps as he came to a screeching halt in front of a pay phone.

"You have reached the Burns residence, we cannot come to the phone right now," said a recording of his wife's voice on the other end of the line.

"Shit...the god damned answering machine," yelled Jason angrily, banging the receiver against the palm of his other hand that was now covered with dried blood.

"At the sound of the beep......"

"Marnie, it's me, you've got to call the cops, a woman was murdered trying to help me! 235 Westwood Street in Brockton...now do you believe me? Marnie, the same bastard who put me out of business and ruined our lives is the same son of a bitch who is trying to kill me... Marn...so I'm fucking crazy?... I'm not fucking crazy! God, Marn...he cut her head off.... He, he cut her god damned head off... Oh, Marnie....call the cops and get the hell out of there...maybe they're watching you now.... I've got to go... I've got to get to Bigelows..." quivered Jason as he slammed the receiver down while covering his mouth with his hand. He felt as though he were going to vomit, so he took in a large gulp of air and wiped the sweat off of his forehead. There was no time for that, he thought as he jumped in the car and turned on the ignition while not realizing that the car was running. A large grinding noise filled the night air. He slammed the gear shift into drive and pushed the gas pedal down to the floor.

His car swayed back and forth as his tires screeched, filling the lot with a cloud of dust and smoke. He took a sharp right at the next intersection and manically weaved in and out of cars on the two lane road. He could see the illuminated Bigelows of Boston sign down the road as he cut in front of a forty-foot semi to avoid a head on collision with another coming in the opposite direction. The night air was filled with the sound of air horns as though the two trucks slowed down and pulled toward the curb...in utter disbelief at what he had just done.

Jason grabbed the steering wheel and yanked it firmly to the left. His car skidded sideways and would probably have flipped if it were not for a patch of sand that now rose like a cloud. He could see smoke and dust in his rearview mirror as he sped toward the pyramid entrance, slammed on his brakes, and ran in.

"Heh, buddy, where's your security pass? Halt... I said halt!" yelled two guards as Jason ran past them and toward the warehouse entrance.

One guard began chasing him while the other ran to the security office.

"Freeze!" yelled the pursuing guard as he unsnapped his holster and removed his 38. "Freeze, or I'll shoot!"

Jason dived onto the tiled hallway floor...arms extended as though he were sliding into home plate. The security guard poised himself, both arms outstretched while holding the pistol with both hands and aiming. He could hear the shot ring out and echo down the long hall way.

The gun recoiled, and a cloud of smoke covered the guard's view. Before it cleared, Jason rolled to his side, leaped up, and ran through the door leading to the warehouse. He ran into the clothing racks as though he were running into a forest. He could hear the warehouse door swing open and slam against the cinder block wall. Jason's body bobbed up and down as he maneuvered his way through the miles of garments that were suspended from long steel pipes. As the guard approached, he pushed the garments aside, held onto the steel pipe, raised his body so that his feet were not be visible, and sandwiched himself in between two long red winter coats. While nestling there among the clothing fauna, trying not to move or breath, suspended like a bat in a cave, the guard walked by.

He waited a few seconds until he felt undetected, then lowered himself and ran in the opposite direction. He pushed garments aside as he cut a path for himself through the thick cloth jungle.

After a few minutes, he stopped pushed some dresses aside and peaked. He found himself next to a clearing near the packing stations.

Running from cover and into the isle and began shouting at the top of his lungs, "Your lives are in danger... Bigelow is going to kill us all tonight! You must leave...or you will all be killed!"

The packers stopped working, poked their heads out of their cubicles, and without saying a word, nervously stared at Jason. Their faces were filled with fear. Suddenly their heads moved from side to side...first to Hess, who was running toward Jason on the right, and then to three security guards...fire arms drawn...who were running toward Jason on the left. All of the security cameras were humming, their little bodies moved back and forth as though they were experiencing some sort of muscle spasm.

"Grab him!" yelled Hess as Jason bolted back into the protection of the surrounding clothes racks.

Jason ran toward the side of the building where he could see the illuminated exit sign beckoning him. He ran toward the door and leaned on the emergency push bar, but the door wouldn't open. He then ran to the next exit door and also found it locked. He turned his head and saw Hess running towards him. Running as fast as he could, he headed back toward the packing stations.

"The emergency doors are locked, you are all going to die here.....if you don't believe me, go and try them!..." he yelled as he ran past the 135 packing stations.

Panic suddenly set in, and as twenty to thirty packers left their stations, viewing their action, the other hundred quickly followed. They all surrounded Jason like Conestoga wagons fending off an Indian attack. Their sheer numbers provided Jason with protection from Hess and the guards. Within a few moments, they stampeded toward the emergency exits, dragging Jason with them.

A number of employees had reached other exits before Jason, and he could hear them yelling in the distance, "The fucking doors are locked...they're locked!"

He could hear the emergency push bars being slammed against metal exit doors. Suddenly someone shrieked, "FIRE! FIRE!" as smoke began filling the warehouse.

Jason looked up and saw smoke bellowing from the overhead ventilation ducts. Thick, heavy smoke quickly fell to the floor like a soupy New England fog, and workers began grabbing their throats gasping and collapsing. He ran to one of the clothing racks, grabbed a garment, covered his mouth with it, and began breathing in shallow gulps of air.

The acrid smoke was now so thick that he could barely see in front of him. A strange sound emanated from the smoke impregnated warehouse as the painful moans of hundreds of workers filled the air. It was a macabre symphony of death.

Jason ran over bodies as he kicked in the chain link door to the maintenance cage and grabbed a section of steel pipe. He then ran to one of the exit doors that was barely visible through the smoke. Lifeless bodies were stacked two and three deep in front of the door, some with blood pouring from their mouths and ears...others with their hands clutched to their throats. Two bodies, with their limp arms still clutching the metal push bar, blocked the door. Jason grabbed their arms and dragged them aside. With steel pipe in hand, he bashed the steel door over and over while holding the garment up to his face with the other. Gasping for air, he noticed a small steel grate on the wall. He felt his strength leaving his body as he stumbled to his knees. His eyes watered from the smoke that now penetrated the garment, filling his lungs and numbing his face and arms.

Knowing that this was his last chance to get out of there alive, he took a deep breath, dropped the garment, and with both hands on the steel pipe, began banging the grate. Slowly at first and then faster and faster, harder and harder until he realized that he could no longer hold his breath. The grate bent and then fell to the floor. While exhaling Jason flung the pipe through the hole, put his arms in front of himself as though he were diving, and leaped through the opening.

He could hear the steel pipe bouncing on the pavement outside while he pulled his feet through the opening. Bending over he took in a number of deep breathes, retrieved the pipe, and began running toward the side of the huge corrugated steel building. He ran as quickly as he could, but his lungs and nostrils were still burning as mucus dripped from his nose and mouth. As he inhaled, his insides felt as though they were on fire. His tongue was extremely sensitive and had swelled slightly. When he approached the corner of the steel building, he could see the small brick structure protruding from its side.

His mind was disoriented, but he felt that it was here that Bigelow had his office. Just before reaching the back entrance to the building, he collapsed from exhaustion. His body moved up and down as he tried to get his breath....he knew what he must do. He attacked the door like a Samurai, violently plunging the steel pipe into the aged wooden door. It easily splintered as he savagely pounded it over and over. Wood and glass fragments filled the air as he swung the pipe like a crazed woodsman.

He then ran through the destroyed frame in the building. No sooner had he entered, the two security guards appeared at the end of the hallway. Both had their guns drawn and both fired at him. His body was thrown backwards from the impact of a bullet that entered his right shoulder.

At first he felt just numbness, but suddenly a surge of excruciating pain engulfed him...it felt like nothing he had ever experienced. The steel pipe rolled out of hand. He lunged for it just as another bullet ricocheted off of the spot he had just occupied. Pieces of vinyl tile shattered like pieces of shrapnel.

As the guards ran towards him, he grabbed the pipe in his left hand and swung it hitting one guard squarely across the knees. He could hear the cartilage breaking as the guard screamed out in pain. The guard collapsed in the path of the other, causing him to trip directly in front of Jason. Jason then quickly raised the pipe above his head, and with a swift chopping motion, hit the side of the guard's head, sending pieces of hair and blood flying in front of him. The guard collapsed, his limpless body crashed as his head hit the vinyl floor.

Jason's shirt was saturated fresh and dried blood. His adrenaline was flowing as he lifted himself, clutching the pipe in one hand and rubbing his bullet wound with the other. He ran toward the black wooden door at the end of the hall and manically began hitting it over and over. The mahogany center panels shattered under his violent blows, leaving only the wooden outer frame. With one strong kick, the remaining frame swung in, slamming against the wainscoting in the mahogany paneled office.

Jason saw the silhouette of a man. His back toward him, seated in front of a wall of color TV monitors...that were sending out a spectrum of bright colors that highlighted his eerie outline. Every screen had images of bodies...in the ladies' room, next to exit doors, in the cafeteria....all lifeless. The cameras were panning back and forth, showing hundreds of lifeless corpses. Many stacked near exits... In spite of all the noise created by Jason in destroying the door and in wheezing as he tried to catch his breath, the man didn't turn around or move. He just sat motionless, staring approvingly at all of the carnage.

The other wall contained floor to ceiling oak shelves that had rows and rows of videos, all neatly stacked. The figure just sat there gazing at the TV monitors, like the devil staring into the fires of hell.

The man then suddenly turned around with a smile on his face and a gun in his hand fired at Jason hitting him in the stomach. With the pipe raised above his head, Jason let out a blood curdling scream and then lunged at him in a Kamikaze fashion. The pipe struck Bigelow on the left temple, causing his hand to fly back while firing a shot into the screen of one of the monitors. The tube exploded, filling the room with a midst of shattered glass and smoke. Bigelow's body fell toward the shelves of video cassettes. Jason grabbed an armful of them and threw them onto Bigelow's head whose eyes were now rolling backwards.

Bigelow suddenly stood up like Lazarus. blood dripping from his head. He reached out for Jason's pipe as he swung it again. Before striking Bigelow on the right side of his head, the pipe struck two video cassettes that somehow remained undisturbed on the shelf as though they were glued there. Bigelow fell to the floor, and the entire shelf began moving sideways...revealing a hidden room.

As the shelf moved sideways, an amber-colored desk lamp across the room switched on, creating an eerie glow. An old Emerson radio sitting on a credenza began playing Glen Miller's, "In The Mood." Everything in the room was covered with cob webs that slowly swayed in the breeze, as though they were moving to the rhythm of the big band music. Jason, grimacing with pain, clutching his stomach, noticed the silhouette of a man sitting at the desk with his back towards him. He could see the top of a brown felt hat above the back of the black leather desk chair.

Jason raised the pipe in his left hand and ran over to the leather chair. He raised the pipe and spun the chair around.

Sitting there fully clothed was a skeleton of a man with cob webs in his eye sockets. Some of his brown mummified flesh still clung to his skull. His tie was still neatly tied to his yellowed shirt while his spinal column supported his white skull.

Jason dropped the pipe, collapsed to the floor, and yelled, "Oh my God... Oh my God...."

While lying there clutching his stomach, he heard footsteps running down the hall.

Using the pipe as a support, he raised himself, stumbled into next room, removed Bigelow's gun from his clenched hand, and pointed it at the smashed office door.

"Don't shoot...police..." yelled two cops who stood in the door way in flack jackets while pointing semi-automatic rifles at him. He dropped the hand gun to the floor and collapsed from the loss of blood.

"Jason....are you alright....Jason," came a familiar voice from the far end of the hall way. Her voice became louder and louder as she ran past the two police officers and took Jason in her arms.

"Marnie, Marnie," whispered Jason, barely audible above the screeching sirens.

She bent over and whispered in his ear, "Jay, I love you, everything is going to be fine, now rest."

He closed his eyes and passed out in her arms. She held his blood-soaked hand, rubbed his forehead, and said, "Yes, Butch, everything is going to be fine."

CHAPTER 12

His tall, slim body was slumped at the end of a long crude wooden table...both arms were folded and rested on the table's edge. Round steel-framed glasses sat mid-point on the bridge of his nose, his gray disheveled hair sloped onto his forehead, nearly touching his salt and pepper eyebrows, his dark green prison shirt was buttoned to his neck.

Aside from the table, chair, bed, sink, and toilet, the room was Spartan. A single overhead incandescent light, covered with wire mesh, cast shadows onto the floor. His only other companions sat perched in the opposite corners of his cell humming and spying. They were not intrusive...they were his friends. Humming like worker bees around their queen...

This grand voyeur euphorically visualized his captors experiencing the same sexual arousal that he felt. Lenses caressing his body and then transporting him to a monitor where he organsmically explodes onto a screen...his naked soul exposed for all to view. He wondered if they were taping him. If they were, then his being would be converted to magnetic impulses, where they would transcend his mortal self and achieve immortality. It would then lay dormant in its plastic case until released again and again like a genie in a bottle.

For security reasons, he was the only prisoner in the entire cell block. After murdering 850 workers, and according to the prosecuting attorney, he was the largest mass murderer in US history. There were calls, even from the most liberal factions, to reinstate the death penalty. Because nearly half of those murdered were minorities, minority leaders; and politicians from around the country called his actions, those of a fanatical racist. Labor unions used the incident as a rallying point to solicit new members so that, as they stated in their monthly newsletter, "An incident such as this is never again perpetrated upon the American worker. If Bigelow's had been unionized, this probably would never had happened."

He knew that they were wrong and was undisturbed by their speculation and sophomoric psychoanalysis. His spirit forever remained an elusive shadow on the walls of his mind. Moving in and out of the light in an abortive attempt at overcoming obstacles and ultimately escaping into a world of love and acceptance.

His inner thoughts at times became so bizarre that even he feared their existence. To him his complex meaning of life was more important than life itself. He felt no remorse because to him, failures deserve neither consolation, nor compassion. To him his life had meaning and purpose. A surgical instrument that is purged of bacterium in an autoclave is regarded as pure and cleansed. There is no remorse for virus that is killed, nor is there praise for the one that has escaped. There is but one emotion. To him love and hate contained the same basic ingredients: a strong emotional expression, a propensity to express that emotion, and a gratification or guilt following its expression. His personality was an emotional caldron that blended all feelings into one puree. In the end, only one thing mattered...just one.

"You've got to find your way alone...you've got to get through it alone," he thought as he stared at his handmade cardboard maze that filled most of the table in front of him.

The hand bent card board twisted and turned and was held together by small pieces of tape and wet toilet paper. He stared intently into the maze and at a small cockroach he had placed at the its entrance.

"Come on, go, you can overcome any obstacle, you must make it through on your own," said Bigelow impatiently as though the bug understood him.

The tiny roach just sat there motionless. Then Bigelow leaned over, and forming his lips as though he were about to whistle, blew some air onto the bug, causing it to wiggle its little antennae. Its tiny body then moved spasmodically along the twisted trail. Scouring and then stopping and scouring again... Before exiting it came to a complete halt...sat their calmly and seemed to be viewing its anticipated newfound freedom.

And then as though propelled by some strange force of fate, it ran out of the maze with its tiny legs moving it forward out into the light.

In one quick motion, Bigelow, with a maniacal smile on his face, raised his hand high above his head and slammed it on to the bug with such intensity that the sound reverberated throughout the entire cell block.